"You...
Bu...

"Primed from an early age to take over Crane Enterprises. It's all you know. That isn't red blood that flows in your veins, but ink from profit and loss statements."

They stopped the pretense of dancing. Caasi had never felt so cold. Shock, hurt and a myriad of emotions came at her from every direction.

Wordlessly she dropped her hands and took a few steps in retreat. The silence between them was charged like the still air before a storm. It was all she could do to turn away and disguise the searing pain that burned through her heart.

Dear Reader:

Welcome to Silhouette Desire – provocative, compelling, contemporary love stories written by and for today's woman. These are stories to treasure.

Each and every Silhouette Desire is a wonderful romance in which the emotional and the sensual go hand in hand. When you open a Desire, you enter a whole new world – a world that has, naturally, a perfect hero just waiting to whisk you away! A Silhouette Desire can be light-hearted or serious, but it will always be satisfying.

We hope you enjoy this Desire today – and will go on to enjoy many more.

Please write to us:

> Jane Nicholls
> Silhouette Books
> PO Box 236
> Thornton Road
> Croydon
> Surrey
> CR9 3RU

The Trouble with Caasi

DEBBIE MACOMBER

SILHOUETTE
Desire

DID YOU PURCHASE THIS BOOK WITHOUT A COVER?

If you did, you should be aware it is **stolen property** as it was reported *unsold and destroyed* by a retailer. Neither the Author nor the publisher has received any payment for this book.

All the characters in this book have no existence outside the imagination of the Author, and have no relation whatsoever to anyone bearing the same name or names. They are not even distantly inspired by any individual known or unknown to the Author, and all the incidents are pure invention.

All rights reserved. The text of this publication or any part thereof may not be reproduced or transmitted in any form or by any means, electronic or mechanical, including photocopying, recording, storage in an information retrieval system, or otherwise, without the written permission of the publisher.

This book is sold subject to the condition that it shall not, by way of trade or otherwise, be lent, resold, hired out or otherwise circulated without the prior consent of the publisher in any form of binding or cover other than that in which it is published and without a similar condition including this condition being imposed on the subsequent purchaser.

First published in Great Britain in 1994 by Silhouette Books, Eton House, 18-24 Paradise Road, Richmond, Surrey TW9 1SR

© Debbie Macomber 1985

Silhouette, Silhouette Desire and Colophon are Trade Marks of Harlequin Enterprises B.V.

ISBN 0 373 59333 3

22-9410

Made and printed in Great Britain

DEBBIE MACOMBER

hails from the state of Washington. As a busy wife and mother of four, she strives to keep her family healthy and happy. As the prolific author of dozens of best-selling romances, she strives to keep her readers happy with each new book she writes.

Other Silhouette Books by Debbie Macomber

Silhouette Special Edition

Starlight
Borrowed Dreams
Reflections of Yesterday
White Lace and Promises
All Things Considered
The Playboy and the
   Widow
°Navy Wife
°Navy Blues
For All My Tomorrows
Denim and Diamonds
Fallen Angel
The Courtship of Carol
   Sommars
†The Cowboy's Lady
†The Sheriff Takes a Wife
°Navy Brat
°Navy Woman
°Navy Baby
‡Marriage of Inconvenience
‡Stand-in Wife
‡Bride on the Loose
Hasty Wedding

+Groom Wanted
+Bride Wanted
+Marriage Wanted

†*The Manning Sisters*
°*Navy Series*
‡*Those Manning Men
   Trilogy*
+*From This Day Forward*

Silhouette Desire

Yesterday's Hero

*Silhouette Christmas
   Stories 1988*
"Let It Snow"

Take Three Women 1994
"The Apartment"

For
Susan and Mark, Nancy and Ken,
Linda and Joe,
for the great weekend in Portland

Chapter One

The majestic beauty of white-capped Mount Hood was unobstructed from the twentieth floor of the Empress Hotel in downtown Portland. Caasi Crane stood in front of the huge floor-to-ceiling window, her arms hugging her slim waist. Blake Sherrill's letter of resignation was clenched tightly in one hand.

Blake was the best general manager she'd ever hope to find. His resignation had caught her off guard. As far as Caasi knew he had been perfectly content. His file lay open on top of her desk, and Caasi moved across the plushly decorated office to study the information.

His salary was generous, she noted, but Caasi believed in paying her employees what they were worth. And Blake earned every cent. Maybe he'd reconsider if she offered him a raise. But according to the file, he'd received a healthy increase only three months earlier.

Flipping through the sheets of paper, Caasi paused to read over the original employment application. Six three and a hundred and eighty pounds. Dark hair and brown eyes. None of that had changed. Unmarried and twenty-eight. Certainly she would know if he'd married, but the application had been filled out—she searched for the date—eight years before. Had Blake been with Crane Enterprises that long? Funny she didn't remember that.

Caasi pushed the wide-rimmed glasses up from the tip of her nose and sat in the cushioned white leather chair.

Her secretary buzzed, interrupting her thoughts. "Mr. Sherrill's here to see you."

Caasi released the intercom lever. "Please send him in." Mentally she prepared herself. Her father had groomed her well for this position. If Blake was displeased about something, she'd find out why. Employee performance and customer satisfaction were the name of the game. But an employee, even one as good as Blake, couldn't perform if he was unhappy. If so, Caasi wanted to know the reason. She pretended an interest in his file when the door opened. Looking up, she smiled brightly. "Sit down, Blake." Her hand indicated a chair on the other side of her desk.

He wasn't a handsome man. His features were rough and rugged, too craggy to be considered urbanely attractive. His chin projected stubbornly and the shadow of his beard was heavy. Caasi didn't doubt that he had to shave twice a day. He wore a dark business suit and silk tie, and his hair was coal dark. Could he be Italian with a name like Sherrill? Funny how she'd never really noticed Blake. At least, not the toughness in the lean, hard figure that stood in front of her.

"If you don't mind, I'd rather stand." With feet braced slightly apart, he joined his hands.

"Honestly," Caasi admonished with a soft smile, "you look like a recruit standing at attention."

"Sometimes I feel that way." The words were hardly above a whisper.

"Pardon?" Caasi looked up again.

"Nothing." The small lines about his eyes and mouth creased in a mirthless smile. "You're right. I'll sit down."

"How long have you been with us now, Blake?"

"Eight years, six months, and five days," he replied drily and took a pack of cigarettes from inside his jacket. "Do you mind if I smoke?"

"You've smoked in here dozens of times. Why ask me now?"

He shrugged. "Maybe I was hoping to gain your attention."

Caasi gave him a troubled look. What was the matter with him? Not in the five years since she'd taken over the company had Blake behaved like this.

"You have my attention now." She held up the resignation letter. "What's the problem?"

He lit his cigarette and inhaled deeply before answering. "There's no problem. The time has come to move on, that's all."

"Is it the money?"

"No."

"Have you got another job?"

"Not yet." He took another drag on the cigarette and flipped the ashes into the glass tray that sat on the corner of her desk.

"Let me have one of those." This wasn't going well and she was fast losing her grip on the situation.

"I didn't know you smoked." Smoldering dark eyes regarded her with surprise.

"I don't, normally." The display of nerves would have been heartily disapproved of by her father, but for once Caasi didn't care. She needed that cigarette.

Blake took the package out of his jacket a second time and handed her one.

Caasi placed it between her lips and half rose from her chair as Blake held his lighter out to her. Her fingers rested lightly over his hand in a guiding gesture and she watched in amazement as his jaw clenched.

Sitting back down, she inhaled and blew the smoke at the ceiling. "All right, Blake, tell me what's up."

"Do you want a full written report? There's one due at the end of the month as usual."

"I don't mean that and you know it." Angrily she ground out the cigarette in the ash tray.

"Damn wasteful," he commented, his eyes on the cigarette. "Supplies would go up ninety per cent if everyone at the Empress—"

"I've never known you to be sarcastic," Caasi cut in.

"But then, you've never known me, have you?"

Caasi didn't know how to answer him. Maybe if she'd dated more often she'd be able to deal with men more effectively. That was one area in which her father had failed to instruct her. Sometimes she felt like a bungling teenager, and just as naïve.

"Take the rest of the week off, Blake. I would like you to reconsider this letter."

"I'm not going to change my mind." There was a determined look about him, unyielding and confident.

She didn't want to lose Blake. "Take it anyway, and let's talk again the first of the week."

He gave her a mocking salute. "As you wish."

Blake's resignation weighed heavily on Caasi the rest of the day. By the time her secretary left, she was in a foul mood. It was due to far more than Blake, she recognized that. That night was the monthly get-together with Edie and June, her two college friends.

The months passed so quickly that sometimes it seemed that they were meeting much too often—and at other times it wasn't nearly enough. Yet the two were her best friends . . . her *only* friends, Caasi admitted grudgingly as she slid the key into the lock of her apartment door.

The penthouse suite on the twenty-first floor had been Caasi's home for as long as she could remember. She must have been eight before she realized that milk came from a cow and not the busboy who delivered all of the family's meals.

Daddy's little girl from the beginning, Caasi had known from the time she could walk that someday she would be president of Crane Enterprises and the string of hotels that ran down Oregon's coast and into California. Isaac Crane had tutored her for the position until his death five years earlier.

Daddy's little girl . . . The thought ran through her mind as Caasi opened her closet and took out a striped dress of teal, plum, and black. Everything about her reflected her father. A thousand times in her twenty-eight years Caasi had explained that her name hadn't been misspelled but was Isaac spelled backwards.

Soaking in a bubble bath a few minutes later, Caasi lifted the sponge and drained the soothing water over her full breasts and flat stomach. Her big toe idly played with the faucet. Her medium-length chestnut hair was piled on top of her head as she lay back and let the hot water refresh her.

Steam swirled around the huge bathroom as Caasi wrapped a thick cotton towel around herself and moved into her bedroom. She didn't feel like going out tonight. A quiet dinner and television would be more to her liking, but she knew Edie and June well enough to realize they wouldn't easily let her forgo their monthly dinner.

An hour later, Caasi entered Brasserie Montmartre, a French restaurant Edie had raved about the previous month. Caasi didn't mind checking out the competition. The Empress's own small French restaurant served some of the best food in town.

Edie waved when she saw Caasi. June apparently hadn't arrived yet, and Caasi wondered if she would, since June's baby was due any time.

"Greetings, fair one," the pert brunette said as Caasi pulled out a chair and sat down. It was a standard joke between them that, of the three, Caasi was the most attractive. She accepted their good-natured teasing as part of the give and take in any friendship. They were her friends, and God knew she had few enough of those these days.

"You look pleased about something," Caasi said. Edie was grinning from ear to ear.

"I am." Edie took a sip of champagne and giggled like a sixteen-year-old. "I should probably wait until June's here, but if I don't tell someone soon, I think I'll bust."

"Come on, give," Caasi urged and nodded at the waiter, who promptly delivered another glass and poured for her. Good service, she mused.

"I'm pregnant!"

Caasi nearly choked on the bubbly liquid. "Pregnant!" she spat back. Not both friends at the same time. It was too much!

"I don't think I've ever seen Fredd more excited."

"But you were the one who said—"

"I know, but I changed my mind. It's crazy, but I'm really happy about it. The doctor said there's no reason for me to lose my figure, and he's already put me on a high-protein diet. Fredd's agreed to the natural childbirth classes. From what we've read it's the best way for the baby. June's taking them now, and I'm hoping she can ask to let me sit in on one of her sessions. And then there's the nursery to do. I think Fredd may make the cradle."

"Slow down," Caasi said with a light laugh. "My head's spinning already."

"What do you think?" Edie scooted back her chair and arched her shoulders.

"Think about what?" Caasi shook her head.

"Do I show?"

"Show? For heaven's sake, Edie, you can't be more than a couple of months along!"

"You're right." She giggled, her dark eyes dancing. "I was just hoping."

"Hoping what?" A tall blond waddled up behind them. June's protruding stomach left little conjecture as to her condition. One hand rested against her rib cage as she lowered herself into the third chair. "Champagne?" Round blue eyes sought those of the others. "What are we celebrating?"

"Babies, in the plural," Edie supplied with a wide grin that lit up her whole face.

June looked blank for a minute.

"It seems our Edie has found herself with child," Caasi informed her.

"Edie?" June whispered disbelievingly. "Not the same Edie who marched in a rally for zero population growth?"

"One and the same." Edie laughed and motioned for the waiter, who produced a third glass.

"We're talking about the girl who was afraid to eat lettuce because it could ruin her perfect figure."

"Not the one who said 'Lips that touch chocolate shall never touch mine'?" June's eyes rounded with shock.

"'Fraid so," Caasi said with an exaggerated sigh.

"Would you two quit talking about me as if I wasn't here?" Edie demanded.

"A baby." Caasi looked from one to the other and shook her head. "Both of you. Wasn't it yesterday that I was your maid of honor, June? And Edie, remember how we argued over who got which bed our freshman year?"

"I always thought you'd be the first one to marry," June said to her in a somber tone. "Caasi the beauty. Gray eyes that mirrored her soul and a figure that was the envy of every girl in school."

"The fair one," Edie added.

"The aunt-to-be," Caasi murmured in a poor attempt at humor. "Always the bridesmaid, never the bride."

"I find it more than just ironic," Edie said with conviction. "It's high time you came down from the lofty twentieth floor and joined us mortals."

"Edie!" June snapped. "What a terrible thing to say!"

"It's the champagne," Caasi said, excusing her friend.

"In this instance it's a case of loose lips sinking ships."

"Ships?" Edie inquired.

"Friendships!"

"To friendship." Edie raised her glass and their former good mood was restored.

"To friendship." June and Caasi gently clicked their delicate crystal glasses against Edie's, and all three sipped the amber liquid.

"By the way, who's paying for this?" June questioned.

"I don't know," Caasi joked, "but I'm only paying one fifth, since both of you are drinking for two."

They all laughed and picked up their menus.

As Edie had promised, the food was superb. With

observant eyes, Caasi noted the texture and quality of the food and the service. Such scrutiny had been ingrained in her since childhood. Caasi doubted that she could dine anywhere and not do a comparison.

"What about next month?" Caasi eyed June's stomach.

"No problem. Doc says I've got a good five weeks."

"Five weeks?" Edie looked shocked. "If I get that big, I'll die."

"You know, Edie, if your shoes are a little too tight, don't worry," Caasi teased.

"My shoes?" Edie looked up with a blank stare.

"After being in your mouth all night, they should fit fine."

Edie giggled and stared pointedly across the table. "I swear, the girl's a real wit tonight."

They divided up the check three ways. Although Caasi wanted to treat her friends, June and Edie wouldn't hear of it.

Sitting back, she watched as the waiter took their checks. No matter what her mood at the beginning of these gatherings, Caasi always felt better afterward. Even Edie's remark had flowed off her like water from an oily surface. These two were like sisters. She accepted their faults and loved them none the less.

Large drops of rain pounded against the street as the three emerged from the restaurant.

"How about an after-dinner drink?" Edie suggested. "I'm in the mood for something sweet."

June and Caasi eyed one another and attempted to disguise a smile.

"Not me." June bowed out. "Burt's at home,

anxiously awaiting my return. He worries if I'm out of his sight more than five minutes."

Edie raised both brows, seeking Caasi's response.

Caasi shrugged. "My feet hurt."

"I thought I was the one with tight shoes," Edie teased, looping her arm through Caasi's. "Come on, be a sport. If you're extra nice I'll even let you take me up to your penthouse suite."

Caasi sighed. "I suppose a hot buttered rum would do wonders toward making me forget my problems."

"What about you, June? Come on, change your mind."

June shook her head and patted her rounded stomach. "Not tonight."

The hotel lobby at the Empress was peacefully quiet when Edie and Caasi came through the wide glass doors. The doorman tipped his hat politely, and Caasi gave him a bright smile. Old Aldo had been a grandfather when the hotel hired him twenty years before. Other employers would have retired him by now, but Caasi hadn't. The white-haired man had a way of greeting people that made them feel welcome. That quality wouldn't easily be replaced.

The sweet, soulful sounds of a Manilow ballad drifted from the cocktail lounge, and Edie paused to hum the tune as they waited for the elevator.

"Nice," she commented.

"The piano player's new this week. Would you rather we had our drink down here?"

Edie's nod was eager. "I think I would. I'm in the mood for romance."

Caasi's laugh was sweet and light. "From the look

of things, I'd say it's been a regular occurrence lately." Her eyes rested on her friend's still smooth abdomen.

The maitre d' seated them and saw to their order personally. The crowd was a good one. Caasi looked around and noted a few regulars, mostly salesmen who stayed at the hotel on a biweekly basis. The after-work crowd had thinned, but there were a few die-hards.

The middle-aged man at the piano was good. A portion of the bar was built around the piano, and Caasi watched as he interacted with the customers, took requests and cracked a few jokes. She'd make sure he was invited back again.

Edie's index finger circled the top of her Singapore sling glass while Caasi's hands hugged her own hot buttered rum. They didn't talk. They didn't need to. The piano music filled the room. A young couple at the bar started to sing and were joined by several others.

Edie's hand squeezed Caasi's forearm. "I'm sorry about what I said earlier."

"No need to apologize." Edie's gaze faltered slightly under Caasi's direct look. "I understand."

A long sip from the clear plastic straw was followed by, "I worry about you sometimes, Caasi."

"Worry about me? Whatever for?"

"I love you. You're more like a sister to me than my own. I don't know how you can be happy living the way you do. It's not natural."

"What's not natural?" Caasi realized she was beginning to sound like a worn echo.

"Your life."

Mildly disconcerted, Caasi looked away. "It's the only way I've ever known."

"That doesn't make it right. Haven't you ever yearned for someone to share your life? A man to cuddle up against on a cold night?"

Caasi's laugh was forced. "I've got my electric blanket."

"What about children?"

Although content with her life-style, Caasi had to admit that seeing both June and Edie pregnant was having a peculiar effect on her. She'd never thought much about being a mother, but, strangely, she found the idea an appealing one. "I . . . I think I'd like that, but I'm not so keen on a husband."

"If it's a baby you want, then find yourself a man. You don't need a wedding ring and a march down the aisle to have a baby. Not these days."

Caasi tugged a strand of hair behind her ear, a nervous habit she rarely indulged. "I can't believe we're having this conversation."

"I mean it," Edie said with a serious look.

"What am I suppose to do? Find a good-looking man, saunter up, and suggest children?"

Edie's full laugh attracted the attention of others. "No, silly, don't say a word. Just let things happen naturally."

How could Caasi explain that she wasn't into casual affairs? Had never had a fling, and at twenty-eight remained a virgin? Edie would be sick laughing. Lack of experience wasn't the only thing holding her back; when would Caasi have had the time? Every waking minute was centered around Crane Enterprises. Even if she did find herself attracted to a man, she'd have to squeeze him in between meetings and conferences. Few men would be willing to accept that kind of relationship. And what man wouldn't be intimidated by her wealth? No, the die had been cast and she . . .

"Caasi." Edie's hushed whisper broke into Caasi's thoughts. "What you need is a man like the one who just walked in."

Caasi's gray eyes searched the crowd for the newcomer. "Where?" she murmured.

"There, by the piano. He just sat down."

The blood exploded in Caasi's cheeks, rushing up from her neck until she felt her face shining like a lighthouse on a foggy night. Blake Sherrill was the man Edie had pointed out. Pressing a tentative hand to her face, Caasi wondered at her reaction.

"Now, *that's* blatant masculinity if ever I've seen it."

"He's not that good-looking," Caasi felt obliged to say, grateful that Edie hadn't noticed the way the color had invaded her face.

"Of course not. His type never is. There's a lean hardness to him, an inborn arrogance that attracts women like flies to honey."

"Oh, honestly."

"Notice his mouth," Edie continued.

Caasi already had. Blake looked troubled about something, a surprising occurence, since he'd always presented a controlled aura when he met with her. She watched as he ordered a drink, then emptied the shot glass in one gulp. That wasn't like Blake either. As far as she knew, he stayed away from liquor.

"See how his lips are pressed together? The tight, chiseled effect. Women go for that."

There was a slight tremor in Caasi's hands as she lifted her drink to her mouth. "Maybe some women. But not me."

"Caasi." Edie groaned. "You can't be *that* stupid. You're staring at an unqualified hunk. Good grief, my blood's hot just looking at him."

"He's not my type," Caasi muttered under her breath, at the same time thinking she'd never really seen Blake. For years they'd worked together, and not once had she ever thought of him except as an exceptionally good general manager.

"That man is every woman's type. I've seen high-society types kill for less."

Caasi knew her friend was teasing and offered a halfhearted smile. "Maybe he is my type, I don't know."

"Maybe?" Edie shot back disbelievingly. "Go over and introduce yourself. It can't hurt, and it may do you a lot of good."

"Do you think I should?"

"I wouldn't have said so if I didn't."

"This is crazy." Caasi shoved back her chair. What did she hope to accomplish? Blake *was* more man than she'd ever recognized before, but the idea of a casual affair with him was crazy. More than crazy, it was ludicrous.

"Hurry up before he leaves," Edie whispered encouragingly.

Caasi didn't know why she didn't want her friend to know she was already well acquainted with Blake.

Edie stood with her.

"Are you coming too?" Caasi cast her a challenging glare.

"Not this time, although I'm tempted. I just noticed the time. Fredd will be worried. I'll call you tomorrow."

"Fine." Caasi's spirits lifted. She could leave without saying a word to Blake and Edie need never know.

"I'll just wait by the door to see how you do. Once you've made the contact, I'll just slip away."

Caasi's spirits plummeted.

The stool beside Blake was vacant. Caasi strolled across the room, her heart pounding so loudly it drowned out the piano man. Setting her drink on the counter, she perched atop the tall stool.

Blake looked over at her, surprise widening his eyes momentarily. He turned back without a greeting.

"'Evening," she muttered, shocked at how strange her voice sounded. "I thought you were taking the rest of the week off."

"Something came up."

Caasi straightened. "What?"

"It's taken care of—don't worry about it."

"Blake." Her tone was crisp and businesslike.

Pointedly he turned his wrist and looked at his watch. "I was off duty hours ago. If you don't mind, I'd like to leave the office behind and enjoy some good whiskey." He raised his shot glass in a mocking toast.

Caasi's throat constricted. "I've had one of those days myself." She didn't mention that his letter had brought it on, but that understanding hung oppressively in the air between them.

The bartender strolled past and braced both hands against the bar. "Can I get you anything?" He directed the question to Caasi.

Obviously he didn't know who she was, which was just as well; she could observe him at work. "I'll have the same as the gentleman."

Blake arched both brows. "It must have been a harder day than I thought."

"It was."

His lips came together in a severe line. "Drink it slowly," he cautioned.

"I can hold my liquor as well as any man." Why was she being so defensive? She didn't want to be. What she wanted was an honest, frank discussion of why he had decided to leave Crane Enterprises.

"As you say." The corners of his mouth curved upward in challenge.

When Caasi's drink arrived she raised it tentatively to her lips and took an experimental sip. To her horror, she started coughing and choking.

"You all right?" he questioned with a rare smile.

As if she wasn't embarrassed enough, his hand pounded vigorously against her back.

"Stop it," she insisted, her eyes watering.

"I thought you said you could handle booze."

"I can!" she choked out between gasps of air. "It just went down wrong, that's all."

Blake rotated the stool so that she was given a profile of his compelling features. He lit a cigarette and took a long puff. Caasi couldn't remember noticing how firm his mouth was until that night. How could she have worked so closely with someone for five years and miss something like that?

She turned back around, aware that half the lounge was watching her.

"Can I borrow one of those?" Caasi asked him after a moment.

"If you're going to take up smoking, the least you can do is buy your own." He took the pack from his pocket and pulled out a cigarette.

"You're right," Caasi murmured with shaky conviction. "I shouldn't. That's one habit I can do without."

"I'm finding I can do without a lot of things."

"You don't have to do without a job," Caasi inserted.

He turned to her then, his eyes dark and glittering as his taut gaze ran over her. "In this instance I do."

"Why?" she queried, her hand curling around the small glass. "At least you owe me the courtesy of telling me why after all these years you want out."

"It's not a marriage, Cupcake."

Caasi bristled. "Don't call me that. Don't ever call me that." Cupcake had been her father's pet name for her. Only Isaac Crane had ever called her that. "I'm not a little girl anymore."

His laugh was short and derisive. "That you're not."

She took another sip of her drink. It burned all the way down her throat and seared a path through her stomach. But she didn't cough and felt pleased with herself.

"What do you want from me?" he asked as he crushed his cigarette in the ashtray with barely suppressed savagery.

Feeling slightly tipsy and more than a little reckless, she placed her hand gently over the crook in his elbow. "I want to dance."

His head jerked up, and the color seemed to flow from his face. "Not with me."

"Yes, with you," she said softly, surprised at how angry he sounded. Who else did he think she meant? The piano player?

"No."

The word was issued with such force that Caasi felt as if he'd physically struck her. Uncharacteristic tears welled in her soft gray eyes, and Caasi knew she had to get out of there before disgracing herself further. What was the matter with her? She hadn't cried since her father's death.

Her hands were trembling as she slid off the stool. Wordlessly she turned and walked out of the lounge. She made it as far as the elevator before the first hot tear ran down her face. She bit the corner of her mouth, hoping to prevent the others from falling. It didn't work.

The penthouse was dark. Very dark. Even the million lights of the city couldn't illuminate the room. Leaning against the door, Caasi heaved her shoulders in a long shuddering sigh. She'd had too much to drink that night, far more than normal. That was what was wrong. Not Edie. Not Blake. Not even her. Only the alcohol.

Undressing, she pulled the long nylon gown over her head. Accidentally, her hand hit against her abdomen and she paused, inhaling deeply. Lightly her fingers traced her breasts, then fell lifelessly to her sides as she hung her head in abject defeat.

"I am a woman," she cried. Sobs racked her shoulders as the tears came from her soul. "I am a woman," she repeated, and fell across the bed.

Chapter Two

Caasi's head throbbed the next morning when the alarm rang. She rolled over and moaned. She'd made a complete idiot of herself the night before. Had she really suggested that Blake take her dancing? Heavens, she hadn't been on a dance floor since her college days. The temptation was to bury her head under a pillow and go back to sleep, but the meeting with Pacific Contractors was scheduled for that morning, plus a labor relations conference for that afternoon.

Louise, the paragon of virtue who served as Caasi's secretary, was already at her desk when Caasi arrived.

"'Morning," Caasi greeted her crisply.

"Schuster's been on the phone twice. He said it's important." Louise held out several pink message slips.

Caasi groaned inwardly. Every time Schuster

phoned it was important. She didn't want to deal with him. Not today. Not ever, if she could help it.

"Is Mr. Sherrill in yet?" Caasi would give the pesky troublemaker to Blake to handle. He'd deal with Schuster quickly and efficiently. Caasi almost groaned out loud when she remembered that she'd given Blake the rest of the week off.

"He's been in and out," Louise announced, following Caasi into the inner office. "He left something on your desk."

A silver tray with a large pot and cup rested on the clean surface of her desk. Beside the cup was a large bottle of aspirin. A hint of a smile touched Caasi's mouth.

"Thanks, Louise," she murmured and waited until the short, plump woman left the office.

A folded piece of paper lay on the tray beside the aspirin. Slowly, Caasi picked it up, her heart hammering wildly. A single note and her heart was reacting more to that than any profit-and-loss statement.

The large, bold handwriting matched the man. How often had she read his messages and not noticed that his penmanship personified him? The note read: *Thought you could use these this morning. B.*

Caasi realized that she could. Snapping the cap off the bottle, she shook two tablets into the palm of her hand and poured the steaming coffee into the cup. She lifted her hand to touch the chestnut hair gathered primly at the base of her neck as she lazily walked across the carpet.

Everything last night hadn't been a fluke. Edie had raised questions that Caasi had long refused to voice.

She was a woman, with a woman's desires and a woman's needs. Home, husband, children—these were things she had shelved. Seeing June and Edie happily married, in love and expecting children, was bringing all these feelings to an eruptive head. Her father hadn't counted on that. Caasi was the only child, the last of the Cranes, who were now an endangered species. With Isaac gone, there was only Caasi. Alone. Against the world.

Caasi wanted to be protected and loved, cherished and worried about. Like Edie and June. But at the same time, she wanted to be proud, independent, strong . . . everything her father had worked so hard to ingrain in her. Sometimes she felt as though a tug of war were going on inside her, with her heart and soul at stake. Some days she looked in the mirror only to discover that a stranger was staring back at her.

The phone buzzed, interrupting her musings. Another day was about to begin, and her doubts would be pushed aside and shelved again.

Saturday morning Caasi woke, sat up in bed, and sighed heavily. The past two days, she'd crawled out of bed more tired than she'd been the night before, as if she hadn't slept at all. Now her eyes burned and she felt as if the problems of the world were pressing against her shoulders.

The company copter was flying in that day, and Caasi was scheduled to officiate at a ground-breaking ceremony at Seaside. Another Empress Hotel, the tenth, was about to be launched. She should be feeling a sense of pride and accomplishment, yet all she felt was tired and miserable. The day would be filled with false smiles and promotional hype.

She dressed in a navy-blue linen suit, double breasted. Her father would approve.

Her breakfast tray was waiting for her, but she pushed it aside and instead reached for a cigarette. After yesterday, she'd broken down and bought a pack. Not that she smoked more than half a cigarette before smashing it out. The cigarette reminded her of Blake. Absent two days and she missed him like crazy. He was scheduled to have gone with her on this little jaunt. Somehow, having Blake along would have made the outing far more endurable.

Caasi was back at her suite by four. Exhausted, she kicked off her shoes and pulled the pins from her hair. The weather was marvelous, a glorious, sunny April afternoon. How could she have felt anything but exhilarated by the crisp ocean breeze? Everything had run smoothly—thanks to Blake, who had been responsible for setting up the ceremony.

The instant his name floated through her mind, the heaviness she'd experienced that morning returned. For years she'd taken him for granted. In rethinking the situation, Caasi realized that he had cause to resign. But he was invaluable to her. He couldn't leave; she wouldn't let him. The sooner he understood her feelings, the better.

Slouching against the deep, cushioned couch, Caasi propped her feet on the shining surface of the glass coffee table. She'd talk to him. Explain Crane Enterprises' position. And the sooner, the better. Now. Why not?

After changing into a three-piece pant suit, Caasi

sailed into her office to look through his personnel file. They'd worked together for years and she didn't even know where he lived. There were so many things she didn't know about Blake.

Her finger ran down the information sheet until she located the Gresham address, several miles outside of Portland.

Her silver Mercedes had been a gift from her father. Caasi had little need to drive it. Usually she made a point of taking it for a spin once a month. It had been longer than that since she'd last driven it, but the maintenance men kept it tuned and the battery charged for her.

It took almost thirty minutes to find the address. She drove down a long, winding road that seemed to lead nowhere. Although there were several houses around, they were separated by wide spaces. Blake . . . in the country. The mental image of him tilling the fields flitted into her mind. The picture fit.

She stopped at the side of the road and, before pulling into Blake's driveway, checked the nearest house number against the one she'd scribbled down in her office. The house was an older two-story with a wide front porch, the kind Caasi would picture having an old-fashioned swing. A large weeping willow tree dominated one side of the front yard. Caasi had always loved weeping willows.

By the time she opened the car door and climbed out, Blake had come out of the garage, wiping his hands on an oily rag.

"Caasi." His voice was deep and irritated.

"Afternoon," she replied, sounding falsely cheerful. "This is beautiful country out here."

"I like it." He came to a halt, still several feet from her.

"Everything went fine today."

"I knew it would."

Caasi untied the lemon-colored chiffon scarf from her throat and stuffed it in her purse. "Can we talk?"

His gaze traveled over her before he lifted one shoulder. "If you like."

Caasi felt some of the tension ease out of her. At least he was willing to discuss things.

"Go in the house; I'll wash up and be there in a minute."

"Okay," she agreed readily.

"The back door's unlocked," he called to her as he returned to the garage.

Caasi let herself into the rear of the house. An enclosed porch and pantry contained a thick braided rug, on which she wiped her feet. The door off the porch led into a huge kitchen decorated with checkered red-and-white curtains on its large windows.

The glass coffeepot resting on the stove was half full, and Caasi poured herself a mug, hugging it to keep her hands occupied.

Her purse clutched under her arm, she wandered out of the kitchen. A large formal dining room contained built-in china cabinets. An array of photographs filled the open wall space. Caasi stopped to examine each one. Had Blake been married? A small frown of nervous apprehension creased her brow. Several pictures of children who vaguely resembled Blake dominated the grouping. Another of an older couple, dark and earthy, captured her attention. Caasi lifted the wooden frame to examine the two faces more closely. His parents? They both had round, dark eyes—wonderful eyes that said so much. Warm, good people. If Caasi ever had the opportunity to meet them, she knew she would love these people. They were the salt of the earth. There was another picture that rested behind the others. This one was of a large family gathering outside what appeared to be the very house she was in. The willow tree was there, only smaller. The two adults were shown with six children. Blake's family. He stood out prominently, obviously the eldest.

"My parents," he explained from behind her.

Caasi hadn't heard him come in and gave a startled gasp, feeling much like a child caught looking at something she shouldn't. Her hand shook slightly as she replaced the photograph.

"The children?" she asked hesitatingly.

"My nieces and nephews."

"You've never married?"

Blake's mouth thinned slightly. "No." He ran a hand through his dark hair. "You said you wanted to talk?"

"Yes." Her head bobbed. "Yes, I do."

"Sit down." His open palm gestured toward the living room.

Caasi moved into the long, narrow living room. A huge fireplace took up an entire wall, and she paused momentarily to admire the oil painting above the mantel. Mount Hood was richly displayed in gray, white, and a forest of green, against a backdrop of blue, blue skies.

"Wonderful painting," she commented casually, looking for the artist's name and finding none.

"Thanks."

Caasi sat in a chair where she could continue to study the mountain scene. On closer inspection she found minute details that weren't readily visible on casual notice. "I really like it. Who's the artist?"

The small lines about Blake's mouth hardened. "Me."

"You!" Caasi gasped. "I didn't know you did anything like this. Blake, it's marvelous."

He dismissed the compliment with a short shake of his head. "There's a lot you don't know about me."

"I'm beginning to find that out," she said on a sober note.

His eyes pinned her to the chair.

Uncomfortable, she cleared her throat before continuing. "As I mentioned, the trip to Seaside went without a hitch. But it didn't seem right, not having you there."

"You'll get used to it."

"I don't want to have to do that."

Blake propelled himself out of the overstuffed chair he had sunk into and stalked to the far side of the room. "My decision's been made."

"Change it."

"No."

"Blake, listen." She set her coffee aside and stood. "Today I realized how inconsiderate I've been the last few years. Putting it simply, I've taken you for granted. You were Dad's right-hand man. Now you're mine. I don't know that I can do the job without you."

His laugh was sarcastic, almost cruel. "I have no doubts regarding your ability. More than once I've been amazed at your insight and discernment. You're one hell of a businesswoman, and don't let anyone tell you different."

"If I'm so wonderful, why am I losing you?"

He didn't answer her.

"I'm prepared to double your salary."

"You overpay me as it is."

She clenched her fist at her side and stared at the oil painting, searching for some clue to the man standing with his back to her. "Then it isn't the money."

"I told you it wasn't." Suddenly he was almost shouting.

"Someone else has made you a better offer. Holiday Inn? Hilton?" *Don't yell at me*, she wanted to cry. They'd never argued. For months on end they'd worked together without saying more than a few necessary words to one another. And suddenly everything was changed.

"Caasi." Her name was issued on a soft groan. "I wouldn't do that to you. I don't know what I'm planning yet, but I won't go to work for the competition."

"What is it you want?" Angrily she hugged her stomach with both arms and whirled around. "I've never known you to be unreasonable."

He was silent for so long, she didn't know whether he intended answering her.

"You can't give me what I want."

"Try me." She turned back to him, almost desperate. Blake was right; she could manage without him. A replacement could come in, be trained, and suffice, but she wanted him. Trusted him.

His dark gaze fell to her mouth. They stood so close that Caasi could see the flecks of gold in his dark irises. A strange hurt she didn't understand seemed to show in them. A desire welled in her to ease that pain, but she didn't know how. Wasn't that a woman's job, to comfort? But then, she was a complete failure as a woman.

He reached out and gently touched the side of her face. A warmth radiated from his light caress. "I was planning to take the summer off. Do some hiking. I've always wanted to climb mountains, especially Rainier."

Sadly, Caasi nodded, her eyes captured by his. "I've never hiked." She laughed nervously. "Or climbed."

"There are lots of things you haven't done, aren't there?" His soft voice contained a note of tenderness. He dropped his hand.

Caasi forced her eyes away. Blake didn't know the half of it. Her gaze fell on the rows of family pictures. "Do . . . do you like children?" Why had she asked him that?

"Very much."

"Why haven't you married and raised a houseful? You've got the room for it here."

"The same reason you haven't, Cupcake."

Caasi bit her tongue to keep from shouting at him not to call her that. The name itself didn't bother her. Nor did she care if he reminded her of her father. What she didn't like was Blake thinking of her as a child.

"For the last several years," he elaborated, "the two of us have been married to Crane Enterprises."

"But you could have a family and still work for me." She was grasping at straws and knew it.

"I'm a little too old to start now."

"Old," she scoffed. "At thirty-six?"

Blake looked surprised that she knew his age.

"I don't want to lose you."

His expression hardened as if her words had displeased him. "I'll walk you to your car."

Perplexed, she watched him move across the room and pull open the front door.

"You're angry, aren't you?"

He forced a long breath. "Yes."

"But why? What did I do?"

"You wouldn't understand."

Her hand sliced through the air. "You keep saying that to me. I'm well above the age of reason. I have even been known to exhibit some intelligence."

"And in other ways you're incredibly stupid," he interrupted harshly. "Now go before I say something I'll regret."

Caasi sucked in her breath. Her shoes made a clicking rattle against the wooden steps as she hurried to her car. She couldn't get away from Blake fast enough.

Still angry and upset, Caasi let herself into the penthouse suite and threw her purse on the bed. Her shoes went next, first the right and then the left. She felt like shouting her frustration aloud.

Dinner arrived and she stared at it with no appetite. No breakfast, a meager lunch, and now dinner held no appeal. She should be starved. Steak, potato and baby white asparagus, eaten alone, might as well be overbaked, dried-out macaroni and cheese. Eating alone hadn't bothered her until that night. Why now?

The portrait of Blake's parents came into her mind.

How easy it was to picture his mother standing in the kitchen with fresh bread dough rising on the counter. Kids eating breakfast and laughing. How could something she'd never known bother her so much? *Children. Family. Home.* Each word was as foreign to her as the moon. Yet she felt a terrible, gnawing loss.

Determinedly she took the crusty French roll and bit into it. Hard on the outside, tender inside, exactly right. It was the only thing in her life that was exactly right.

The phone buzzed, which usually meant trouble. Caasi heaved an irritated sigh and lifted the receiver.

"Mr. Sherrill's on his way up," the hotel receptionist informed her cheerfully.

"Thank you," Caasi answered in a shaky voice. Blake coming here? He'd never been to her private quarters. Maybe when her father was alive, but not since she'd taken over.

Hurriedly she rushed into the bathroom and ran a brush through her hair. Halfway out the door, she whirled around and added a fresh layer of light pink gloss to her lips. Her hands shook, she was rushing so much. She unscrewed the cap from a perfume bottle and added a touch of the expensive French fragrance behind each ear and to the pulse points at her wrists.

Caasi started at the sound of his knock. Pausing to take in a deep, calming breath, she sauntered to the door.

"Why, Blake, what a pleasant surprise," she said sweetly.

He didn't look pleased. In fact, he looked much the same as he had when she'd left him earlier.

The feeling of happy surprise drained out of her.

"Go on, change."

"Change?" She stared at him blankly as he walked inside.

"Clothes," he supplied.

"You're not making any sense."

"Yes I am," he refuted. "What you had on last night will do."

"Do for what?" His attitude was beginning to spark her anger.

"Dancing. That's what you said you wanted."

Hot red color extended all the way down her neck. "That was after several drinks."

"You don't want to dance? Fine." He lowered himself onto the long couch. "We can sit and drink."

The dark scowl intimidated her. She'd stood up to angry union leaders, pesky reporters, and a thousand unpleasant situations. Yet one dark glower from Blake and she felt as though she could cry. Her gaze was centered on the carpet, and she noted that in her rush she'd forgotten to put on shoes.

"Caasi?" His voice pounded around the room like thunder.

"I don't know how to dance," she shouted. "And don't yell at me. Understand?" Humiliating tears were misting her eyes, and that angered her all the more. "The last time I went to a dance I was a college sophomore. Things . . . have . . . changed."

She moved to the window and pretended an interest in the city lights.

Blake moved behind her and gently laid a hand on her shoulder. "What you need is a few lessons."

"Lessons?" she repeated softly. The image that

came to her mind was of the times the hotel had booked the ballroom for the students of the Arthur Murray and Fred Astaire dance studios.

"I'll be your teacher." The words were husky and low-pitched. The gentle pressure of his hand turned her toward him.

Submissively, Caasi's arms dangled at her sides. "What about music?"

"We'll make our own." He began to hum softly, a gentle ballad that the piano man had played the night before. "First, place your arms around my neck." Lightly his hands rested on the curve of her hip just below her waist.

Caasi linked her fingers behind his neck. "Like this?"

Their eyes met and he nodded slowly—very slowly, as if the simple action had cost him a great deal. The grooves at the sides of his mouth deepened and he drew her close. His hands slid around to the small of her back, his touch feather-light.

Caasi had to stand on the tips of her toes to fit her body to his. When she eased her weight against him he went rigid.

"Did I do something wrong?" she asked in a whisper.

"No." His breath stirred her hair. "You're doing fine."

"Why aren't we moving?"

"Because it feels so good just to hold you," he said in a strange, husky voice.

A flood of warmth filled every pore, and when she raised her eyes she saw that his angry look had been replaced by a gaze so warm and sensuous that she went completely still. She didn't breathe. She didn't move. She didn't blink.

He moved his hand up her back in a slow, rotating action that brought her even closer, more intimately, against him.

"Blake?" Her voice was treacherously low.

His other hand slid behind her neck, and he wove his fingers into her hair. "Yes?" Slowly, Blake lowered his mouth, claiming the trembling softness of hers.

His lips were undemanding, the pressure light and deliciously seductive. But soon the pressure deepened, as if the gentle caress wasn't enough to satisfy him.

Caasi's body surged with a warm, glowing excitement. She'd been kissed before, but never had she experienced such a deep, overwhelming response. Her arms locked around his neck, and she moved her hips against him sensuously.

"Caasi . . ." He ground out her name on a husky breath. He kissed her again, and she parted her lips in eager welcome. Their mouths strained against one another, seeking a deeper contact.

Blake tore his lips away and buried his face in her soft throat.

Caasi sighed softly. "My goodness," she whispered breathlessly, "that's some dance step."

Blake shuddered lightly and broke the contact. "Go change, or we'll be late."

"Be late?" she asked, and blinked.

His fingers traced the questioning creases in her brow, then slid lightly down the side of her cheek and under her chin. "My cousin's wedding is tonight. If we hurry we'll make it to the dance."

"Will I meet your family?" Somehow that seemed important.

"Everyone. Even a few I'd rather you didn't know."

"Oh, Blake, I'd like that," she cried excitedly. "I'd like that very much."

Blake smiled, one of those rare smiles that came from the eyes. He had beautiful eyes, like his parents, and Caasi couldn't move. His look held her softly against him.

"Hurry," he urged in a half groan.

Reluctantly she let him go and took a step in retreat. "Are you sure what I wore last night will be all right? I have plenty of more formal outfits."

"It's fine. But whatever you wear, make sure it has a high neckline."

"Why?" she asked with a light laugh.

"Because I don't want any of my relatives ogling you." He sounded half angry.

Hands on her hips, her mood gay and excited, Caasi laughed. "Honestly, there isn't that much to ogle at."

Boldly, his gaze dropped to the rounded fullness as he studied her with silent amusement. "You have ten minutes. If you haven't appeared by that time, I'll come in and personally see to your dress."

The threat was tempting, and with a happy sigh, Caasi hurried out of the room.

Sorting through her wardrobe, she took out a pink-and-green madras skirt and top. The blouse had a button front, so the option of how much cleavage to reveal was left strictly to her. Purposely she left the top three buttons unfastened, blatantly revealing the hollow between her breasts. Caasi realized she was openly flirting with Blake, but she hadn't flirted with anyone in so long. The desire to do so overrode her usual modesty.

Blake was standing at the window looking out when she appeared. He turned and froze, his gaze meeting hers.

"Will I do?" Suddenly she felt uncertain. Idly her fingers played with the buttons of her blouse, fastening the most provocative one.

"Dear God, you're beautiful."

Caasi felt a throb of excitement pulsate through her. "So are you."

The intensity of his look deepened, and he glanced at his watch. Caasi had the impression he couldn't have told her the time if she'd asked.

"We'd better go."

"I'll get a jacket." Cassie returned to her bedroom and took a black velvet jacket from the hanger.

Blake took it out of her hand and held it open, gliding the soft material up her arms. His hands cupped her shoulders and brought her back against him. His breath stirred the hair at the crown of her head.

The sensations Blake was causing were new. So new that Caasi hadn't time to properly examine them. Not then. Not when his hand held her close to his side as they took her private elevator to the parking garage. Not when he opened the passenger door of the '57 T-Bird with the convertible top down. Not when he leaned over and lightly brushed his mouth across hers.

The dance was held in a V.F.W. hall off Sandy Boulevard. The lot was full of cars, the doors to the huge building open while loud music poured into the night.

"Once you meet my relatives you might consider yourself fortunate to be getting rid of me."

Caasi wished he hadn't mentioned his resignation but forced herself to smile in response. "Do you think I could find your replacement here?"

Either he didn't hear the question or chose to ignore it.

"Hey, Blake, who's the pretty lady?" A couple of youths strolled toward them. Caasi could remember trying to walk in the same "cool" manner.

The boy who had spoken was chewing a mouthful of gum.

"You toucha' my lady and I breaka' your head." Blake's teasing voice carried a thread of warning.

Caasi doubted that either boy took him seriously.

"These two are my baby cousins."

"Baby cousins." The boys groaned. "Hey, man, give us a break."

"You taking your lady to Rocky Butte?" The second youth was walking backward in front of Blake and Caasi, his arms swinging at his sides.

"Rocky Butte?" Caasi glanced up at Blake.

"The local necking place." His hand found hers, and Caasi enjoyed the sensation of being linked to this powerful man. "You game?"

"No," she said, teasing. "I want more dancing lessons."

His chuckle brought an exchange of curious glances between the youths.

"You're not going to dance, are you, Blake? That's for sissies."

"Wait a few years," he advised. "It has its advantages."

They paused in the open doorway. The polished wooden floor was crowded with dancing couples. A five-piece band was playing from a stage to the far right-hand side of the hall. Long tables containing food were against another wall, and several younger children were helping themselves to the trays of sweets. Older couples sat talking in rows of folding chairs.

A sense of wonder filled Caasi. This was a part of Blake. A part of life she had never experienced. "Are you related to all these people?"

"Most of them."

"But you know everyone here?"

"Everyone." He looked down at her and smiled. "Come on, I want you to meet my parents."

As soon as people were aware that Blake had arrived, there were shouts of welcome and raised hands. He responded with his own shouts, then gave Caasi a whispered explanation as to various identities.

"How many uncles do you have?" she asked, astonished.

"Ten uncles and twice as many aunts. I gave up counting cousins."

"It's marvelous. I love it." Her face beamed with excitement and the laughter flowed from her, warm and easy.

Blake stopped once and turned her around, placing a hand on each shoulder. "I don't think I've ever heard you laugh. Really laugh."

She smiled up at him. "I don't know that I have. Not in a long time."

The bride, in a long, white, flowing gown, the train wrapped around her forearm, giggled and hurried to Blake. "I didn't think you'd ever get here," she admonished and stood on tiptoes to kiss his cheek. "Now you have to dance with me."

Blake laughed and cast a questioning glance at Caasi. "Do you mind?"

"No, of course not." She stepped aside as Blake took the young woman in his arms. A wide path was cleared as the couple approached the dance floor. People began to clap their hands in time to the music.

Someone bumped against Caasi, and she turned to apologize. "Sorry," she murmured.

The dark eyes that met hers were cold and unfriendly. The lack of welcome surprised Caasi.

"So *you're* the one who's ruined my brother's life!"

Chapter Three

"Ruined your brother's life?" Caasi repeated incredulously. "I'm Caasi Crane." The girl obviously had her confused with someone else. A curious sensation attacked the pit of Caasi's stomach at the thought of Blake with another woman.

"I know who you are," the woman continued in angry, hissing tones. "And I know what you've done."

What she'd done? Caasi's mind repeated. Those same wonderful eyes that had mesmerized her when she had studied the photo of Blake's parents were narrowed and hard in the tall woman beside her. Blake's own eyes darkened with the same deep intensity when he was angry.

"Are you sure you're talking to the right woman?"

"Oh, yes, there's no doubt. I'd know you . . ."

Loud applause prevented Caasi from hearing the rest of what the woman was saying.

Caasi watched as the young bride, laughing and breathless, hugged Blake. His eyes were full of amusement, but when his gaze found Caasi and saw who was with her, the humor quickly vanished. He kissed the bride, handed her to the waiting groom, and hurried across the crowded dance floor to Caasi's side.

"I see Gina has introduced herself to you," Blake said as he folded an arm around Caasi's shoulder. He smiled down at her, but there was a guarded quality in his gaze.

The eyes of the two women clashed. Something unreadable flickered in Gina's. Surprise? Warning? Caasi didn't know.

"We didn't get around to exchanging names," Caasi said as she held out her hand to Blake's sister. It was important to clear away the misconception Gina had about her.

The hesitation was only minimal before Gina took her hand and shook it lightly.

"If you'll excuse us," Blake said, directing his comment to his sister, "I want to introduce Caasi to Mom and Dad."

"Sure," Gina said, her voice husky. She cleared her throat and shook her head as if to dispel the picture before her. Her look was confused as she glanced from her brother to Caasi. "I'm sure they'd like that."

"I know I would." Caasi didn't need to be a psychic to feel the finely honed tension between brother and sister. That Gina adored him was obvious just by the way she was looking at him. That same reverence had been in the eyes of the young bride. Blake was an integral part of this family, loved and respected. Caasi, on the other hand, belonged to no one; her life had never appeared so empty—just a shell. She'd give everything she owned—the hotels, her money, anything—to be a part of something like this, to experience that marvelous feeling of belonging.

Blake was watching her, his look curious. "You look a hundred miles away."

"Sorry," she answered with a feeble smile.

He escorted her to a row of folding chairs. Several older women were gathered in a circle and were leaning forward, chatting busily.

"Mother." Blake tapped one of the women gently on the shoulder and kissed her cheek affectionately.

"Blake!" his mother cried in a burst of enthusiasm as she stood and embraced her son. "You did come! I knew you wouldn't disappoint Kathleen."

The gray-haired woman had changed little from the photo Caasi had seen. Although several years older and plumper, Blake's mother was almost exactly the same. Warmth, love, and acceptance radiated from every part of her. Caasi had recognized those wonderful qualities in the photo; in person they became even more evident.

"Mother." Blake broke the embrace. "I'd like you to meet Caasi Crane." He turned to Caasi. "My mother, Anne Sherrill."

"Miss Crane." Two large hands eagerly enveloped Caasi's. "We've heard so much about you. Meeting you is a long-overdue pleasure."

"Thank you," Caasi replied with a wide smile. "I

feel the same way." She couldn't take her eyes from the older woman. "You're very like your photo."

Anne Sherrill looked blank.

"I should explain," Caasi inserted quickly. "I was at Blake's house this afternoon."

"Where's Dad?" Blake's arm continued to hold Caasi to his side. She enjoyed the feeling of being coupled with him, the sense of belonging.

Anne Sherrill clucked with mock displeasure. "In the parking lot with two of your uncles."

Fleetingly Caasi wondered what they were doing in the parking lot but didn't ask.

Blake's rich laughter followed. "Do you want me to check on him for you?"

"And have you abandon Miss Crane?" Mrs. Sherrill sounded outraged.

"Please, call me Caasi," was Caasi's gentle request. "I don't mind." The latter comment was directed at Blake. "I'll stay here and visit with your mother. I wouldn't mind in the least."

"I'll only be a few minutes," Blake promised. "Mom, keep Caasi company, and for heaven's sake, don't let anyone walk away with her." He kissed his mother on the cheek and whispered something about lambs and wolves. With a knowing smile, his mother nodded.

Caasi had to bite her tongue to keep from asking what the comment had been about.

"Have you eaten?" Anne wanted to know. "With that son of mine, you probably haven't had a chance to breathe since you walked in the door. Let's fix you a plate. Not fancy food, mind you."

Caasi started to protest but realized she *was* hungry. No, starved. "I'd like that," she said as she followed Blake's mother to the row of tables against the wall. The variety of food was amazing, and all home-cooked, from the look of the dishes. It was probably a pot-luck supper, with each family contributing. Thick slices of ham, sausage, and turkey and a dozen huge salads were set out, along with several dishes Caasi didn't recognize.

Anne handed Caasi a paper plate and poured herself a cup of punch.

"This looks fantastic," Caasi murmured as she surveyed the long tables. She helped herself to a slice of ham and a couple of small sausage links. The German-style potato salad was thick with bacon and onions, and Caasi spooned a small serving of it alongside the ham. "This should be plenty."

"Take as much as you like. There's always food left over, and I hate having to take anything home with me."

"No, no, this is fine. Thank you."

They sat down again. Caasi balanced her plate on her knees and took a bite of the potato salad. "This is really delicious." The delicate blend of flavors wasn't like anything she'd ever tasted.

"Anne's German potato salad is the best this side of heaven," the middle-aged woman on the other side of Caasi commented.

"You made this?" Caasi looked at Anne.

Anne nodded with a pleased grin. "It's an old family recipe. My mother taught me, and now I've handed it down to my daughters."

Anne Sherrill's heritage to her daughters included

warmth, love, and recipes. Caasi's was a famous father and a string of hotels, but given the chance she'd gladly have traded.

"No one makes German-style potato salad like Anne," the other woman continued. When she paused, Anne introduced the woman as Blake's cousin's wife.

"What's in it?" Caasi questioned before she lifted the fork to her mouth. Her interest was genuine.

Anne ran down a list of ingredients with specific instructions. Nothing was listed in teaspoons; it was all in dashes and sprinkles. Caasi doubted that the family recipe had ever been written down. Caasi had never known her own mother and at times when growing up had felt a deep sense of loss—but never more than right now. Her father had tutored her so thoroughly in the ways of business and finance. It was only at times like this that Caasi realized how much she missed a mother's loving influence.

"It's best to let the flavors blend overnight."

Caasi picked up on the last bit of information and nodded absently, her thoughts a million miles away.

"You must come to dinner some Sunday."

"I'd like that," Caasi said. "I'd like it very much."

"This is the first time Blake's brought a woman to a family get-together, isn't it?" The cousin's comment came in the form of a question. "Handsome devil, Blake Sherrill. I've seen the way women chase after him. Yet he's never married."

"No, Blake's my independent one."

Caasi paid an inordinate amount of attention to cutting the ham slice. "Why hasn't he married?"

The hesitation was slight. "I'm not really sure,"

Anne supplied thoughtfully. "He loves children. I think he'd like a wife and family, but he just hasn't found the right woman, that's all."

Caasi nodded and lifted a bite of meat to her mouth.

"Is tomorrow too soon?" Anne questioned and at Caasi's blank look continued, "For dinner, I mean."

Mentally Caasi went over Sunday's schedule. It didn't matter; she could change whatever had been planned. "I'd enjoy nothing more. What time would you like me?"

Anne wrote the address and time on the back of one of Caasi's business cards. She wasn't sure why Blake's mother had invited her, but it didn't matter—she was going. Being with his family, Caasi couldn't help but learn more about the enigmatic man who was leaving her just when she was beginning to know him.

"I think I see Blake coming now," Anne murmured with a tender smile. "With his father in tow."

Caasi studied the gentle look on the older woman's face before scanning the room for Blake. She could barely make out his figure through the crowd of dancers. The faint stirrings of awareness he awakened within her surprised Caasi. She was proud to be with Blake, to meet his family, to be included in this celebration.

Their eyes sought one another when he stepped into full view. Hers were soft and welcoming; his, slightly guarded.

"Dad, this is Caasi."

Blake's father reached down and took Caasi's hand,

his dark eyes twinkling. "Pretty thing." The comment was made to no one directly.

"Thank you," Caasi murmured and blushed.

"Fine bone structure, but a little on the thin side. Always did like high foreheads. It's a sign of intelligence."

"Dad." Blake's low voice contained a thin note of warning.

"George." Anne slipped an arm around her husband's waist. "His tongue gets loose after a beer or two," Blake's mother explained to Caasi.

"Would you like to dance?" A corner of Blake's mouth tilted upward. He looked as if dancing was the last thing he wanted.

"If you like." Caasi would have preferred to stay and talk more with his parents, but she recognized the wisdom of following Blake onto the polished floor.

The band was playing a polka, and with a quick turn, Blake pulled her into his arms.

Caasi let out a small cry of alarm. She didn't know how to dance, especially a polka.

"Just follow me," he instructed. "And for heaven's sake, don't step on my toes with those high heels."

"Blake," she pleaded breathlessly, "I can't dance. I don't know how to do this."

"You're doing fine." He whirled her around again and again until she was dizzy, her head spinning with the man and the music.

They stopped after the first dance, and Blake brought her a glass of punch. Caasi took one sip and widened her eyes at the potency of the drink.

"Rum?" she quizzed.

"And probably a dab of this and that."

"Old family recipe," she said with a teasing smile. "I'm getting in on several of those tonight. Oh, Blake, I like your family."

"They're an unusual breed, I'll say that." His voice was lazy and deep.

"Is Sherrill a German name?"

"No. Dad's English, or once was. Mom's the one with the German heritage."

The band started playing a slow waltz, and Caasi's eyes were drawn to the dance floor again.

Blake took the cup from her and set it aside. "Shall we?" His eyes met hers, the laughter gone, as he skillfully turned her into his arms.

A confused mixture of emotions whirled in her mind as he slid his arms around her waist, the gentle pressure at the small of her back guiding her movements.

A warmth flowed through her, beginning at his touch and fanning out until she could no longer resist and closed her eyes to its potency.

Caasi placed her head on his shoulder, her face against his neck. The scent of his aftershave attacked her senses. She was filled with the feel and the smell of Blake. It seemed the most natural thing in the world for her tongue to make a lazy foray against his neck, to taste him.

"Caasi." He groaned. "You don't know what you're doing to me."

"I do," she said with a deep sigh. "And I like it. Don't make me stop."

He brought her closer to him, the intimate feel of his body sensuously moving with hers enough to steal her breath.

"This is insane," Blake ground out hoarsely, as if her touch was causing him acute pain.

Gently his mouth nibbled at her earlobe, and red-hot sensations shot through her like a bolt of lightning. "Blake," she pleaded. "Oh, Blake, this feels so good."

Abruptly he broke the contact and led her off the dance floor. "Just how much have you had to drink?" he demanded roughly.

Caasi was too stunned to answer. She opened her mouth but found herself speechless. Angrily she clamped it closed. The hot color that filled her face only served to anger her more.

"Apparently not nearly enough." Why was Blake acting like this? How could he turn from a gentle lover to a tormenting inquisitor in a matter of seconds?

They stood only a few feet apart, glaring at one another. Neither spoke.

"Hey, Blake, when you going to introduce me to your lady?" A low masculine voice broke into the palpable silence that stretched between them.

A tall, good-looking man with a thick mustache over a wide smile came into view. He was about Blake's age and good-looking in a stylish sports coat. His tie had been loosened, revealing curling black hairs at the base of his throat.

"Johnnie—Caasi. Caasi—Johnnie. My cousin."

Johnnie chuckled, his eyes roaming over Caasi with obvious interest. "You don't sound so thrilled that we're cousins." The comment was directed at Blake, but his eyes openly assessed Caasi.

"I'm not," Blake stated bluntly. "Now, if you don't mind, Caasi and I are having a serious discussion."

"We are?" she interrupted sweetly. "I thought we were through. I was just saying how thirsty I am and how delicious the punch is."

Johnnie cocked his head in gentlemanly fashion. "In which case, allow me to escort you to the punch bowl."

"I'd like that."

"Caasi." Blake's low voice was filled with challenge. "I wouldn't."

"Excuse me a minute, Blake," she returned, ignoring his dark, narrowed look. She placed her arm through Johnnie's offered elbow and strolled away. She didn't need to turn around to see that Blake's eyes were boring holes into her back.

"Like to live dangerously, don't you?" Johnnie quizzed with a good-natured grin.

Caasi's lower lip was quivering, and she drew in a shaky breath. "Not really."

"Then I'd say you enjoy placing others in terminal danger. My life wouldn't be worth a plugged nickel if Blake could find a way of getting hold of me without causing a scene."

The thought was so outrageous that Caasi felt her mouth curve with amusement. "Then why are you smiling?" she asked. Johnnie was obviously a charmer, and she found that she liked him.

"I have to admit," he said with a low chuckle, "it feels good to do one up on Blake. He's the family hero. Everyone looks up to him. Frankly, I'm jealous." Johnnie said it with such devilish charm that Caasi couldn't prevent a small laugh.

"Are you thirsty, or was that an excuse to put old Blake in his place?" he queried.

"An excuse," she murmured wickedly.

"Then let's dance."

Caasi hesitated; dancing with Johnnie was another matter altogether. "I'm not sure."

"Come on," he said encouragingly. "Let's give Blake a real taste of the green-eyed monster."

By this time Caasi was beginning to regret her behavior. She was acting like a spoiled child, which undoubtedly confirmed what Blake thought of her.

"I don't think so. Another time."

"Don't look now," Johnnie whispered, "but Blake's making his way over here, and he doesn't look pleased. No," he amended, "he looks downright violent."

Caasi shifted restlessly. The sound of Blake's footsteps seemed to be magnified a thousand times until it was all she could do not to cover her ears.

"Excuse us," Blake said to Johnnie and gripped Caasi's upper arm in a punishing hold, "but this dance is ours."

Caasi glanced at him nervously, resisting the temptation to bite into her bottom lip as he half dragged her onto the dance floor.

When he placed his arms around her the delicious sensations didn't warm her, nor did she feel that special communication that had existed between them only a few minutes previously.

Caasi slid her arms around his neck, her body moving instinctively with his to the rhythm of the slow beat. She studied him through a screen of thick lashes. His mouth was pinched and angry. The dark eyes were as intense as she'd ever seen them, and his clenched jaw seemed to be carved in stone.

Swallowing her pride, Caasi murmured, "I've only had the one glass of punch. I apologize for going off with your cousin. That was a childish thing to do."

Blake said nothing, but she felt some of the anger flow out of him. His arm tightened around her back. "One drink?" he retorted, his mouth moving disturbingly close to her ear.

"Honest."

"You were playing with fire, touching me like that. The way your body was moving against mine . . ." He paused. "If you aren't drunk, then explain the seduction scene." The harshness in his voice brought her head up and their eyes met, his gaze trapping hers.

"Seduction scene?"

"Come on, Caasi, you can't be that naïve," he muttered drily. "The looks you were giving me were meant for the bedroom, not the dance floor."

Her eyes fell and she lost her rhythm, faltering slightly. "Let me assure you," she whispered hotly, hating the telltale color that suffused her face, "that was not my intention."

"Exactly," Blake retorted. "You don't need to explain, because I know you."

"You know me?" she repeated in a disbelieving whisper.

"That's right. You're a cool, suave, sophisticated businesswoman. Primed from an early age to take over Crane Enterprises. It's all you know. That isn't red blood that flows in your veins; it's ink from profit-and-loss statements."

They stopped the pretense of dancing. Caasi had

never felt so cold. Shock, hurt, and a myriad of emotions came at her from every direction.

Wordlessly she dropped her hands and took a few steps in retreat. Her knees were trembling so badly she was afraid to move. The silence between them was charged like the still air before a storm. It was all she could do to turn away and disguise the searing pain that burned through her heart. Blindly she walked off the dance floor.

Somehow she made her way into the ladies' room. Her reflection in the mirror was deathly pale, her blue-gray eyes haunted.

Her hands trembled as she turned on the faucet and filled the sink with cold water. A wet paper towel pressed to her cheeks seemed to help.

Blake was right. Hadn't she recognized as much herself? She wasn't a woman, she was a machine, an effectively programmed, well-oiled machine. How many times had her father warned her against mixing business with pleasure? Enough for her to know better than to become involved with Blake. Why had she come tonight? Where was the common sense her father had instilled in her? And why did the truth in Blake's accusations hurt so much? A hundred questions and doubts buzzed around her like swarming bees.

The sound of someone coming into the room caused Caasi to straighten and make a pretense of washing her hands. She didn't turn around, not wanting to talk to anyone.

"I'm glad I found you." The soft, apologetic voice spoke from behind.

Caasi raised her head and her eyes met Gina's in the mirror. The dark-haired girl looked embarrassed and disturbed. Caasi looked away; she wasn't up to another confrontation.

"I'd like to apologize for what I said earlier," Blake's sister said softly. "It was unforgivable."

Caasi nodded, having difficulty finding her voice. "I understand. It's forgotten." She forced a wan smile to her lips.

"Mom said you're coming to dinner tomorrow."

Caasi's eyes widened; she'd forgotten the invitation. "Yes, I'm looking forward to it."

"I hope we can be friends. Maybe we'll get a chance to visit more tomorrow." Gina offered her a genuine smile as Caasi dried her hands.

With most of her poise restored, Caasi returned to the crowded hall. She saw Blake almost immediately. He stood by the exit, smoking. He jerked the cigarette to his mouth, inhaled deeply, then threw it to the ground and savagely stamped it out.

Caasi made her way across the room to Blake's mother. Anne looked up and a frown marred her brow.

"I enjoyed meeting you, Mrs. Sherrill."

"Anne," the woman corrected softly. "Call me Anne."

"I'd be honored."

"Is something wrong, Caasi?"

Caasi had always prided herself on her ability to disguise her emotions. Yet this woman had intuitively known there was something troubling her.

"I'm fine, thanks. I'll be at your home tomorrow if the invitation's still open."

"Of course it is."

"Say good-night to your husband for me, won't you?"

Anne's eyes were bright with concern. "You do look pale, dear. I hope you're not coming down with something."

Caasi dismissed the older woman's concern with a weak shake of her head. "I'm fine."

Blake had lit another cigarette by the time she came to the front door.

"You're ready to go?" he asked, his tone curt.

"Yes," she said primly. "I'm more than ready."

He led the way to his car, opened her door, and promptly walked around the front and climbed into the driver's side. The engine roared to life even before Caasi could close her door.

The night had grown cold, and Caasi wrapped her arms around herself to ward off the unexpected chill. Maybe it wasn't the night, Caasi mused, but the result of sitting next to Blake. If this cold war continued, she could get frostbite.

They hadn't said a word since they'd left the reception. Caasi couldn't bear to look at him and closed her eyes, resting her head against the seat back.

The wind whipped through her hair and buffeted her face, but she didn't mind—and wouldn't have complained if she had.

The car slowed and Caasi straightened, looking around her. They were traveling in the opposite direction from the Empress. The road was narrow and curving.

"Where are we going?" she asked stiffly.

"To Rocky Butte."

"Rocky Butte?" she shot back incredulously. "Are you crazy?"

"Yes," he ground out angrily. "I've been crazy for eight years, and just as stupid."

Caasi watched as his eyes narrowed on the road. "You're taking me to the local necking place? Have you lost your senses?"

Blake ignored her.

"Why are you bringing me here?" she demanded in frustration. "Do you want to make fun of me again? Is that how you get your thrills? Belittling me?"

Blake pulled off to the side of the road and shoved the gears into park. The challenge in his chiseled jaw couldn't be ignored.

"Remember me?" she said bravely. "I'm the girl without emotions. The company robot. I don't have blood, that's ink flowing through me," she informed him as unemotionally as possible. To her horror, her voice cracked. She jerked around and folded her arms across her breast, refusing to look at him.

Blake got out of the car and walked around to the front, apparently admiring the view of the flickering lights of Portland. Caasi stayed exactly where she was, her arms the only defense against the chill of the late night.

Blake opened her car door. "Come on."

Caasi ignored him, staring straight ahead.

"Have it your way," he said tightly, slamming the door and walking away.

Stunned, Caasi didn't move. Not for a full ten seconds. He wouldn't leave her there, would he?

"Blake?" She threw open the door and hurried after him. Running in her heels was nearly impossible.

He paused and waited for her.

"Where are you going?" she asked once she reached him.

"To the park. Come with me, Caasi." The invitation was strangely entreating. "I've dreamed about having you here with me."

Would she ever understand this man? She should be screaming in outrage at the things he'd said to her and the way he'd acted.

A hand at her elbow guided her up two flights of hewn rock steps to a castlelike fortress. The area was small and enclosed by a parapet. There were no picnic tables, and Caasi wondered how anyone could refer to this as a park. Even the ground had only a few patchy areas of grass.

The light of the full moon illuminated the Columbia River Gorge far below.

"It's beautiful, isn't it?" Caasi whispered, not really sure why she felt the need to keep her voice low.

"I love this place," Blake murmured. "It was too dark for you to notice the rock embankment on the way up here. Each piece fits into the hillside perfectly without a hair's space between the rocks. That old-world craftsmanship is a lost art. There are only a few masons who know how to do that kind of stonework today."

"When was it built?" Caasi questioned.

"Sometime during the Depression, when President Roosevelt implemented the public-work projects."

Despite her best effort, her voice trembled slightly. "You said you'd dreamed of having me here. Why?"

He shot her a disturbing look, as if unaware he'd said as much. "I don't know." He spoke softly, his smoldering gaze resting on her slightly parted lips. He turned toward her, his eyes holding her captive. "I suppose I should take you home."

Caasi's heartbeat soared at the reluctance in his voice. She didn't want to go back to the empty apartment, the empty shell of her life. Blake was here and now and she wanted him more than she'd ever wanted anything in her life.

"Blake . . ." His name came as a tormented whisper.

A breathless, timeless silence followed as he slipped his arms around her. Ever so tenderly, with a gentleness she hadn't expected from him, Blake fit his mouth over hers. Again and again, his mouth sought hers until Caasi was heady with the taste of him.

He moaned when her tongue outlined the curve of his mouth, and his grip tightened. Caasi melted against him as his hands slid down her hips, holding her intimately to his hard body.

Her hands were pressed against the firm wall of his chest and his heartbeat drummed against her open palm, telling her that he was just as affected as she. He felt warm and strong, and Caasi wanted to cry with the wonder of it.

Reluctantly, he tilted his head back, and his warm gaze caressed her almost as effectively as his lips had.

"Shall we go?"

Caasi fought the catch in her voice by shaking her head. If it was up to her they'd stay right there, exactly as they were, for the rest of their lives.

His hand at her waist led her back to the parked car. He lingered a moment longer than necessary after opening her door and helping her inside.

THE TROUBLE WITH CAASI

Blake dropped her off in front of the Empress. "I won't see you inside," he stated flatly.

"Why?" She tried to disguise the disappointment in her voice.

His fingers bit into the steering wheel. "Because the way I feel right now, I wouldn't be leaving until the morning. Does that shock you, Caasi?"

Chapter Four

Caasi checked the house number written on the back of her business card with the one on the red brick above the front door. Several cars were in the driveway as well as along the tree-lined street. Caasi pulled her silver Mercedes to the curb, uneasily aware that her vehicle looked incongruous beside the Fords and Volkswagens.

This was a family neighborhood, with wide sidewalks for bicycle riding and gnarled trees meant for climbing. Caasi looked around her with a sense of unfamiliarity. Her childhood sidewalks had been the elevators at the Empress.

Children were playing a game of tag in the front yard; they stopped to watch her curiously as Caasi rang the doorbell, her arms loaded with a huge floral bouquet.

THE TROUBLE WITH CAASI

"Hi," a small boy called out. His two front teeth were missing and he had a thick thatch of dark hair and round brown eyes.

"Hi," Caasi said with a wide smile.

"I'm Todd Sherrill."

"I'm Caasi."

"Are you coming to visit my grandma?"

"I sure am."

The door opened and Gina called into the kitchen, "Mom, it's Caasi." Gina held open the screen door for her. "Come on in, we've been waiting for you."

"I'm not late, am I?" Caasi glanced at her watch.

"No, no."

Anne Sherrill came into the living room from the large kitchen in the back of the house. She was wiping her hands on a flowered terrycloth apron. "Caasi, we're so pleased you could come."

"Here." Caasi handed her the flowers. "I wanted you to have these."

Anne looked impressed at the huge variety of flowers. "They're beautiful. Thank you."

For all the cars parked in the front of the house, the living room was empty. Caasi glanced around as Anne took down a vase from the fireplace mantel. The decor was surprisingly modern, with a sofa and matching love seat. The polished oak coffee table was littered with several magazines.

"Come back and meet everyone," Anne said encouragingly. "The men are involved in their card game and the women are visiting."

"Which is a polite way of saying we're gossiping," Gina inserted with a small laugh.

Caasi followed both women into the kitchen, immediately adjacent to which was a family room filled to capacity. Children were playing a game of Monopoly on the floor while the men were seated at a table absorbed in a game of cards.

A flurry of introductions followed. Caasi didn't have trouble remembering names or faces; she dealt with so many people in a hundred capacities that she'd acquired skill for such things.

Five of the six Sherrill children were present. Only Blake was missing. Caasi talked briefly with each one and after a few questions learned who was married to whom and which child belonged to which set of parents. Blake and Gina were the two unmarried Sherrill children. But Gina proudly displayed an engagement ring. Caasi's eyes met Gina's. Whatever animosity had existed between them in the beginning was gone. Several grandchildren crowded around Anne and Caasi, following them as Anne led the way outside so that she could show off her prize garden.

"Roses," Gina supplied. "My mother and her roses. Sometimes I swear she cares as much about them as she does about us kids."

"Portland is the City of Roses," Anne said as she strolled through the grounds pointing out each bush and variety of rose as if these, too, were her children.

The bigger grandchildren followed them, while Gina carried a two-year-old on her hip. Young Tommy had just gotten up from his nap and was hiding his sleepy face against his aunt's shoulder.

Todd, the eight-year-old who had introduced himself at the front of the house, linked his hand with Caasi's.

"You're pretty," he commented, watching her closely. "Are you my aunt?"

"Does this mean only pretty girls are your aunts?" Caasi teased him, enjoying the feeling of being a part of this gathering.

Todd looked flustered. "Aunt Gina's pretty, and Aunt Barbara's pretty."

"Then you can call me Aunt if you want to," Caasi told him tenderly. "But I'll have to be a special aunt."

"Okay," he agreed readily. They heard another boy calling him, wanting Todd to play. Todd looked uncertain.

"It's all right, you can go," Caasi assured him. "I'll stay with your grandma, and you can come see me later."

The brown eyes brightened. "You'll be here for dinner?"

"Yup."

"Will you play a game of Yahtzee with me afterwards?"

"If you like."

"'Bye, Aunt Caasi."

Todd's words sent a warm feeling through her. She watched him run off and her heart swelled. This was the first time anyone had ever called her aunt.

The baby in Gina's arms peeked at Caasi, eyeing her curiously.

"Do you think he'll let me hold him?" she asked Gina, putting her hands out to the baby. Immediately, Tommy buried his face in Gina's shoulder.

"Give him a few minutes to become used to you. He's not normally shy, but he just woke up and needs to be held a few minutes."

"Is Donald coming?" Anne asked Gina.

"He'll be here, Mom; you know Donald. He'll probably be late for his own wedding, but I love him anyway."

"Have you set a date?" Caasi questioned as they strolled back to the house.

"In two months."

"The wedding shower's here next month, Caasi. We'd be honored if you came." Anne extended the invitation with an easy grace that came from including everyone, as she probably had all her life, Caasi realized.

"I'd love to. In fact, if you'd like, I could arrange to have the shower at the hotel. I mean, I wouldn't want to take over everything, but that way . . ." She hesitated; maybe she was offending Anne by making the offer.

"You'd do that?" Gina asked disbelievingly.

"We wouldn't want you to go through all that trouble." Anne looked more concerned than dismayed that Caasi would take on the project.

"It's something I'd enjoy doing, and it would be my way of thanking you for today."

"But we can't let you . . ."

"Nonsense," Caasi interrupted brightly, enthusiasm lighting up her expression. "This will give Gina and me a better chance to get acquainted."

"Oh, Mom," Gina said and sighed happily. "A wedding shower at the Empress."

"We'll get together one day soon and make the arrangements," Caasi promised.

Tommy was studying her more intently now. "Can

THE TROUBLE WITH CAASI 71

you come and see me, Tommy?" Caasi asked encouragingly, holding out her hands to him. The little boy glanced from Caasi to Gina, then back to Caasi, before holding out both arms to her.

"You are such a good boy." Caasi lifted him into her arms. She was sure that at one time or another in her life she'd held a small child, but she couldn't remember when, and she thrilled to the way his tiny hands came around her neck.

"I think you've got yourself a friend for life." Anne laughed and held open the back door for Caasi to come inside. Donald had arrived, and Gina hurried into the living room to greet her fiancé.

Tommy's mother was busy making the salad at the sink, and she smiled shyly when Caasi entered the house carrying Tommy.

"Here." Anne pushed out a tall stool for Caasi to sit on while she put the finishing touches on the meal.

Although Caasi joined in the conversation around her, she was enjoying playing peekaboo and pattycake with Tommy. The little boy's giggles rang through the house.

Her face flushed and happy, Caasi glanced up and saw Blake standing in the doorway of the kitchen. He was watching her, and her breath caught in her throat at the intensity of his gaze. At first she thought he was angry. His eyes had narrowed, but the glint that was shining from them couldn't be anger. A muscle worked in his jaw and his eyes seemed to take in every detail of her sitting in his mother's kitchen, bouncing a baby on her lap.

One of his brothers slapped Blake across the back

and started chatting, but still Blake didn't take his eyes off her.

She broke the contact first as Tommy reached for her hair, not liking the fact that her attention had drifted elsewhere. Suddenly a dampness spread through her linen skirt and onto her thighs. She gave a small cry when she realized what had just happened. Laughing, she handed Tommy to his embarrassed mother, who was apologizing profusely.

Anne led Caasi into the bathroom and gave her a dampened cloth to wipe off her teal blue skirt. Someone called Anne and she left Caasi standing just inside the open bathroom door. Amusement lifted the corners of Caasi's mouth into a smile.

"What are you doing here?" Blake was leaning against the door jamb. That warm, sensuous look was gone, replaced with something less welcoming.

"Your mom invited me last night," she told him, her eyes avoiding his as she continued to rub at her skirt. "Do you mind? I'll leave if you do. I wouldn't want to interfere with your family. I'm the outsider here."

He was silent for a long moment.

"No," he murmured at last, "I don't mind."

Some of the tension eased out of her. "If you'll excuse me, I'll see if I can help in the kitchen." She laid the cloth on top of the clothes hamper and started out the door. But Blake's arm stopped her.

"How'd you sleep last night?" A strange smile touched the curve of his mouth. His eyes hardened.

Caasi didn't know what he wanted her to say. "Fine. Why?" she asked tightly.

He shrugged, giving the impression of nonchalance.

THE TROUBLE WITH CAASI 73

"No reason." But he didn't look pleased with her response and turned abruptly to leave her.

Anne gave her the job of dishing up the home-canned applesauce, dill pickles, and spicy beets. All the women were in the kitchen helping in one capacity or another. Laughing and joking with everyone, Caasi didn't feel the least like a stranger. She was accepted, she was one of them. It was the most beautiful feeling in the world.

After the meal, everyone pitched in and helped with the dishes. As promised, Caasi played Yahtzee with Todd and a couple of the other children. Blake was playing cards with his father and brothers and future brother-in-law.

While the children were watching television, Caasi joined the women, who were discussing knitting patterns and recipes. Caasi listened with interest, but her studied gaze was on Blake. He looked up once, caught her eye, and winked. Her heart did a wild somersault and she hurriedly glanced away.

"What game are the men playing?" Caasi asked Gina, who was sitting beside her.

"Pinochle. Have you ever played?"

Card-playing was unheard of in the Crane family; even as a child Caasi had never indulged in something her father considered a waste of valuable time.

"No." Caasi shook her head with a sad smile.

"You've never played pinochle?" Gina repeated incredulously. "I thought everyone did. It's a family institution. Come on, let Dad and Blake teach you."

"No . . . no, I couldn't."

"Sure you could," Gina insisted. "Donald, would you mind letting Caasi sit in? She's never played."

Blond-headed Donald immediately vacated his chair, holding it out for Caasi.

Standing, Caasi looked uncertain. Her eyes met Blake's, but he ignored the silent entreaty. He didn't want her to play, and his eyes said as much. He scooted out of his seat, offering to let another of his brothers take his place.

Caasi felt terrible. The other women hadn't played.

"Come on. I'll coach you," Gina persisted and straddled a chair beside Caasi's at the table.

Cigarette smoke was thick around the area. The other men didn't look half as obliging as Donald, but one look told her he had been losing. Slowly she lowered herself into the vacant seat opposite Blake's father, who was to be her partner.

The cards were dealt after a thorough review of the rules. Gina wrote down the necessary card combinations on a piece of paper as a ready reminder for Caasi. The bid, the meld, and the passing of cards were all gone over in careful detail until Caasi's head was swimming.

They played a practice hand to let Caasi get the feel of the game. Her eyes met Gina's before every move. Once she threw down the wrong card and witnessed her partner's scowl. Caasi's stomach instantly tightened, but George glanced up and offered her an encouraging smile. They made the bid without the point she had carelessly tossed the opponent, and all was well again.

Soon Caasi found herself relaxing enough to enjoy the game. Although playing cards was new to her, the basic principle behind the game was something she'd been working with for years. She studied her opponent's faces when they bid and instinctively recognized what cards were out and which ones she needed to draw. By the time they finished playing, almost everyone else had left—including Blake—and it was almost midnight.

Anne and George walked Caasi to her car, extending an open invitation for her to come again the next week.

"You do this every Sunday?"

"Not everyone makes it every week," Anne was quick to inform her. "This week was more the exception. Everyone was home because of Kathleen's wedding."

Caasi was glad Anne had reminded her. She snapped open her purse and took out an envelope. "Would you give this to Kathleen and her husband for me?" She had written out a check and a letter of congratulations.

"You didn't need to do this," Anne said, fingering the envelope.

"I know," Caasi admitted freely, "but I wanted to."

"I'll see that she gets it."

Caasi could see the elderly couple in her rearview mirror as she drove away. Their arms were around one another as they stood in the light of the golden moon as if they had always been together and always would be. A love that spanned the years.

Caasi was humming as she walked into her office the following morning. Louise, her secretary, gave her a funny look and handed her the mail.

Caasi sorted through several pieces as she sauntered into her portion of the office. Pivoting, she came back to Louise's desk.

"I'd like you to make arrangements for a wedding shower in the Blue Room a week from Thursday. Also, would you send the chef up here? I'd like to talk to him personally about the cake and hors d'oeuvres."

Louise looked even more perplexed. "I'll see to it right away."

"Thanks, Louise," Caasi said as she strolled back into her office.

The morning passed quickly, and Caasi ate a sandwich for lunch while at her desk. She hadn't seen Blake all morning, which wasn't unusual, but she discovered that her thoughts drifted to him. She wondered what he'd say when she did see him. Would he be all business, or would he make a comment about her visit with his family?

She stared down at the half-eaten sandwich and nibbled briefly on her bottom lip. His mother and sister had been discussing a quiche recipe that had been in Wednesday's paper. Caasi hadn't thought much about it at the time, but the urge to bake something was suddenly overwhelming. She'd taken cooking while in high school, but that seemed a hundred years ago. There was a kitchenette in her suite, although she'd never used the stove for anything more intricate than instant coffee. The oven had never been used, at least not by her. There hadn't been any reason to. And even if she did make the quiche she'd be eating it all week.

Still . . .

Impulsively she buzzed her secretary. "Louise, please get me last Wednesday's paper."

Louise returned twenty minutes later looking slightly ruffled as she handed Caasi the newspaper.

Caasi spread it across her desk and pored over it until she found what she wanted. Reading over the list of ingredients, she realized that not only would it be necessary to shop for the groceries, but she would need to buy all the equipment, including pots, pans, dishes, and silverware. Quickly she made out a list and handed it to Louise, who stared at it dumbfounded.

"What you can't find and have delivered to my suite, get from Chef," Caasi instructed on her way out the door to a meeting.

Louise opened and just as quickly closed her mouth, then nodded.

"Thanks," Caasi said.

She was late getting back to her office. Louise had left for the day, but Caasi wanted to check over the list of phone messages before heading upstairs. She was shuffling through the pink slips when she walked into her office and found Blake pacing the floor.

He took one look at her and angrily crushed his cigarette out in her desk ashtray.

"Hello, Blake." She smiled nervously, avoiding his piercing glare. "Is something the matter?" The atmosphere in the room was oppressive. He turned away, his back rigid. "Blake, what's wrong?"

He spun around, obviously angry as his blazing gaze seared over her. "I got a call from my mother this afternoon. She dropped off the card you gave her for Kathleen." His words were harsh. "What the hell is the idea of giving them a check for two hundred and fifty dollars?" The challenge in his eyes was as hard as flint.

Caasi swallowed tightly. "What do you mean?"

"They're strangers to you."

"They're not strangers," she contradicted him sharply. "I met them when I was with you Saturday night. Don't you remember?"

"Kathleen and Bob don't need your charity." His eyes were as somber as they were dark.

"It wasn't charity," she shouted. Her hands shook, and she clenched them into hard fists at her sides. "I have the money. Good Lord, have I got money. What does it matter to you what I do with it?"

"It matters," he shouted in return. "Do you think you can buy yourself a family? Is that it? Are you so naïve as to believe that people are going to love and respect you because of your money?"

Caasi blanched, her hand shooting out behind her to grip the edge of her desk. She suddenly needed its support to stand upright. From somewhere she found the courage to speak. "I don't need anyone, least of all you. Now I suggest you get out. I'll send a letter of apology to your cousin. It wasn't my intent to offend her or you or anyone. Now kindly leave."

He hesitated as if he wanted to say something more, but then he pivoted sharply and stalked out of the room.

Caasi lowered herself into her desk chair and covered her face with her hands. She took several deep breaths and managed to keep the tears stinging the back of her eyes at bay. Was that what Blake honestly thought of her? And his family? The thought was too humiliating to consider. She wouldn't go to the next Sunday family dinner. Maybe that had been Blake's intent all along.

She stayed a few minutes longer in her office, but any thoughts of returning her phone messages had been sabotaged by Blake's anger. She leaned against the elevator wall on the ride to the penthouse suite, weary and defeated. Blake was right in some ways. That was what hurt so much. No matter how much she tried, she wasn't going to fit into the homey family scene with love and acceptance. She didn't belong. Tears blurred her vision as she let herself into the empty suite, and she hated herself for the weakness. What she needed was a hot bath, an early dinner, and bed.

Dinner. . . . Her mind stumbled over the word. She'd canceled her meal for the evening because she'd planned to bake the quiche. The laugh that followed was brittle. Well, why not? She could cook if she wanted to. Who was to care?

Louise had done her job well, and the kitchen was filled with the necessary equipment. After a quick survey, Caasi slipped off her high heels and tucked her feet into slippers. Fearing she'd spill something on her suit, she used an old shirt as an apron, tying the sleeves around her slim waist. Rolling her sleeves up to her elbows, she braced both hands on the counter and read over the recipe list a second time. Lastly, she lined the ingredients up on the short counter top in the order in which she was to use them.

The pie crust was going to be the most difficult; everything else looked fairly simple.

Blending the flour and shortening together with a fork wasn't working, so Caasi decided to mix it with her fingers, kneading the shortening and flour together in the palms of her hands.

The phone rang; she stared at the gooey mixture on her hands and decided to let it ring. Ten minutes later, just as she'd spread a light dusting of flour across the counter and was ready to roll out the dough, there was a loud knock on her door.

"Come on, Caasi, I know you're in there."

Blake.

Panic filled her. He was the last person she wanted to see, especially now.

"Aldo says you haven't left. Your car's in the garage and there's no one in the office, so either let me in or I'll break down the damn door."

He didn't sound in any better mood then he had when she'd last seen him.

"Go away," she shouted, striving—vainly—for a quiet firmness.

"Caasi." His low voice held a note of warning.

"I'm . . ." She faltered slightly with the lie. "I'm not decent."

"Well, I suggest you cover yourself, because I'm coming through this door in exactly fifteen seconds."

She caught her lower lip in her teeth and breathed in deeply. Damn! Why was it that everything in her life had to end up like this?

"It's unlocked," she muttered in defeat.

Blake let himself in, then stopped abruptly when he saw her framed in the small kitchen. A smile worked its way across his face, starting with crinkling amusement at his eyes and then edging up a corner of his chiseled mouth.

"Just what are you making?" he asked, hands on his hips.

"What the hell do you think you're doing, coming up to my suite like this? I should have the security men throw you out on your nose."

"Why didn't you?" he challenged.

"Because . . . because I had dough on my hands and would have gotten it all over the phone."

"That's a flimsy excuse."

Caasi released a low, frustrated groan. "Listen, Blake, go ahead and laugh. I seem to be a source of amusement where you're concerned."

"I'm not laughing *at* you." The humor drained out of his eyes, and he dropped his hands.

"Then say what you came to say and be done with it. I'm not up to another confrontation with you." Her voice was trembling and her eyes had a wild look. Blake had the ability to hurt her, and that was frightening.

"To be honest," he murmured gently as he took several deliberate steps toward her, "I can't recall a time I've seen you look more beautiful."

For every step he advanced, she took one in retreat, until she bumped against the oven door. The handle cut into the backs of her thighs.

"There's flour on your nose," Blake told her softly.

Caasi attempted to brush it aside and in the process spread more over her cheek.

His gaze swept over her and he shook his head in dismay. "Here, let me."

"No." She refused adamantly. "Don't touch me, Blake. Don't ever touch me again."

He looked as though she'd struck him. "I've hurt you, haven't I, Cupcake?" he asked gently.

"You can't hurt me," she lied. "Only people who mean something to me have that power."

He frowned, his dark eyes clouding with some unreadable emotion. *Surely not pain,* Caasi mused.

"For what it's worth," he said quietly, "I came to apologize."

She shrugged, hoping to give the impression of indifference.

"I got halfway home and couldn't get that stricken look in your eyes out of my mind."

"You're mistaken, Blake," she said pointedly, struggling to keep her voice steady. "That wasn't shock, or hurt, or anything else. It was . . ." She stopped abruptly when he placed the tips of his fingers over her lips. Helplessly, she stared at him, hating her own weakness. By all rights she should have him thrown out after the terrible things he'd said.

His hands slid around her waist and she tried to push him away, getting dough on his suede jacket.

"I told you not to touch me," she cried. "I knew something like this would happen. Here, I'll get something to clean that."

"There's only one thing I want," Blake murmured softly, pulling her back into his arms. His mouth settled hungrily over hers.

Caasi's soft body yielded to the firm hardness of his without a struggle. His arms tightened around her waist until every part of her came into contact with

THE TROUBLE WITH CAASI 83

him. For pride's sake, Caasi wanted to struggle, but she was lost in a swirling vortex of emotion. She could feel the hunger in him and knew her own was as strong.

His teeth gently nibbled on her bottom lip, working his way from one corner of her mouth to the other. Caasi wanted to cry at the pure sensuous attack. No one had ever kissed her like that. What had she missed? All these years, what had she missed? Her breath came in quick, short gasps as she broke out of his arms. Tears filled her eyes until he became a watery blur.

"Don't," she whispered achingly and jerked around, her back to him as she placed her hands on the counter to steady herself.

His ragged breathing sounded in her ear as he placed a comforting hand on her shoulder. "That's the problem," he said quietly. "Every time I touch you it nearly kills me to let you go. Someday you won't send me away, Cupcake."

"Don't call me that. I told you before not to call me that."

The phone rang and she glanced at it guiltily, not able to answer it with her dough-covered hands.

"Aren't you going to answer it?" Blake demanded.

She waved a floury hand in his direction.

"Wash your hands. I'll get it for you."

Because the water was running in the sink, Caasi didn't hear what Blake said or who was on the line.

"It's someone by the name of June. She sounded shocked that a man would answer your phone."

Caasi threw him an angry glare and picked up the receiver. "Yes, June."

"Who was that?" June demanded in low tones.

"My general manager. No one important." Caasi smiled at Blake sweetly, hoping the dig hit its mark.

"I just got out of the doctor's office and he said that everything is looking great. He also said that I could have someone in the delivery room with me when my time came, and I was wondering if you'd like to be there."

Caasi didn't even have to think twice. "I'd love to, but what about Burt?"

"Oh, he doesn't mind. I think this is something new the hospital is trying out. I can have two people with me, and I wanted you to be one of them."

"I'm honored."

"I'm going to be touring the hospital facilities on Friday. Could you come?"

"Yes; that shouldn't be any problem. I'll phone you in the morning once I've had a chance to check my schedule."

"I'll let you get back to that unimportant, sexy-sounding manager."

Caasi laughed lightly, knowing she hadn't fooled her intuitive friend. "Talk to you tomorrow," Caasi promised and hung up.

When she returned to the kitchen, she discovered that Blake had taken off his jacket, rolled up his sleeves, and was placing the pie crust into the pan with the ease of an expert.

"Just what do you think you're doing?" she demanded righteously.

"I figured you couldn't possibly eat all this yourself and you'd probably want to invite me to dinner."

"You have a high opinion of yourself, Blake Sherrill."

His boyish smile would have disarmed a battalion. "And if you plan to invite me to dinner, the very least I can do is offer a hand in its making."

Chapter Five

"Well, don't just stand there," Blake insisted. "Beat the eggs."

Caasi hesitated, her feelings ambivalent. She wanted to tell Blake to leave, to get out of her life. He had hurt her in a way she had never expected. But at the same time he had awakened her to what it meant to be a woman, and she wanted him there. He made her laugh, and when he touched her she felt more alive than she had in all her twenty-eight years.

Not fully understanding the reasons why, Caasi decided to swallow her pride and let him stay. She took the eggs and cracked them against the side of the bowl one by one. Silently they worked together. Caasi whipped the eggs until they were light and frothy while Blake chopped onion and green pepper and sliced zucchini.

"I'm going to the hospital Friday," Caasi mentioned casually.

Blake paused and turned toward her. "Is something wrong?"

"No," she assured him quickly. "It's one of the most natural things in the world. Babies usually are."

A stunned silence crackled in the tension-filled room. "Did you say 'baby'?"

Caasi was enjoying this. "Yes," she murmured without looking up, pouring the milk into the measuring cup.

"Are you trying to tell me you're pregnant?" Blake demanded.

Caasi had trouble keeping a smile from forming. "I'm not trying to tell you anything. All I did was make a casual comment about going to the hospital Friday."

"Because of a baby?"

Caasi nodded. She could see the exasperation in his expression.

Blake's eyes raked over her, and she noticed the way the paring knife was savagely attacking the green pepper. "Who's the father?"

"Burt."

"Who the hell is Burt?"

"June's husband."

"But that was June on the phone and. . . ." Blake stopped in midsentence, as comprehension leapt into his eyes. "You little tease," he said deeply, "I should make you pay for that."

"Tease? Me?" Caasi feigned shock. "How could you accuse me of something like that? You have to remember, I'm not a real woman, with real blood."

Blake linked his arms around her waist and nuzzled her neck. "I don't know, you're becoming more approachable by the minute."

"You think so, do you?" A throb of excitement ran through her at his touch. Fleetingly Caasi wondered why she hadn't experienced these sensations with other men.

"Yes, I do." He turned her into his arms, linking his hands at the small of her back. Hungrily, his gaze studied her.

Caasi gave a nervous laugh and broke free. These feelings Blake was creating within her were all too new, too strong. They frightened her.

"I want you to know," Caasi began, taking a shaky breath, "I thought about what you said at the dance—about having ink in my veins."

A silence seemed to fill the small kitchen. "And?" Blake asked her softly.

"And I think you're probably right. Ever since Dad died, I've been so busy with Crane Enterprises that I've allowed that role to dominate my life." She slipped the onion and other vegetables he had chopped into the egg mixture and poured it over the thinly sliced zucchini already in the pie crust. "June and Edie tried to tell me the same thing," she said and gave a weak laugh. "Edie said what I needed was an affair."

"An affair," Blake repeated slowly, his dark eyes unreadable. "So that's what this is all about."

"What?"

"You heard me. What happened then? Did you suddenly look at me and see the most likely candidate?" His words were as cold as a bitter blast of wintry air.

"Of course not. I thought Edie was nuts. I'm not the type of woman who would have an affair. Do you honestly think I'd do something like that?"

"Why not? I won't be around much longer. You can have your fling and be done with me."

Words momentarily failed her as she struggled to control her outrage. "Why do you do this to me? I started out by telling you that you were right in what you'd said about me and suddenly I'm on the defensive again." One hand gripped the oven door, and she knotted the other until the long nails bit into her palm. "June and Edie had noticed that I have no life except the business. All I'm saying is that I'm trying to change that." Irritated with her inability to explain herself in simpler terms, Caasi walked across the suite to stand in front of the large picture window. Her arms hugged her stomach. Did change make her vulnerable to the pain Blake inflicted? If so, she wanted no part of it.

He came to stand beside her but made no attempt to touch her. "Have you noticed how we can't seem to be together anymore without fighting?"

"Oh, yes, I've noticed." Her hands dropped to tight fists at her side.

"By all rights you should throw me out."

Caasi knew that, but she didn't want him to leave. He might have the power to wound, but just as strong was his ability to comfort and heal.

"I can't do that." A wry smile twisted her mouth. "You made half the dinner." It didn't make sense,

Caasi realized, but she wanted him there, liked having him around.

"Truce, Caasi?" His voice was soft and gruff at the same time.

"For how long?" They hadn't gone without fighting for more than a few minutes lately.

"Just tonight. We can get through one night without arguing."

Caasi resisted the temptation to slip her arms around him. "Working together, we can manage it." They'd been a team for years—but soon that, too, would change. The thought was a forceful reminder that Blake had turned in his resignation and would be leaving her soon. She wondered if she'd ever see him again after he left the Empress. The realization that she might not produced a painful sensation in the area of her heart. Blake had always been there. She relied on him. Nothing would be the same after he left. But she couldn't mention that now. Not when they'd agreed on a truce. Every time she said something about him leaving, they fought.

"The quiche has to bake for an hour. Would you like to listen to some music?"

"And have a glass of wine."

Caasi kept a supply of her favorite Chablis available and brought down two crystal glasses. While she poured, Blake inserted a cassette into the tape player.

Music filled the suite as Caasi brought their drinks into the living room.

Blake sat on the couch, holding out his arm to indicate he wanted her at his side. Caasi handed him the wine and sat next to him on the plush leather sofa, leaning her head against his shoulder. A hand cupping her upper arm kept her close. Not that Caasi wanted to be any place else.

The music was mellow and soft, the ballad a love song. Often times, after a long day, Caasi would sit with her feet propped up on the coffee table, close her eyes, and let the music work its magic on her tired body. But the only magic she needed that night was Blake.

"June asked me to go into the delivery room with her when her baby is born," Caasi said, elaborating on the earlier conversation. "That's why I'm going to the hospital this Friday. They want to familiarize the three of us with the procedures."

"Three of you?"

"Four, actually," Caasi said, correcting herself. "Burt, June, baby, and me."

"You're sure you want to do this?" Caasi felt his gaze wandering over her as if in assessment. "From what I understand, labor is no picnic, and for someone who's never had a baby it may be more than you can handle."

Caasi stiffened, biting back angry words. "I want to be there and nothing's going to stop me."

Blake glanced at his wristwatch. "Twenty minutes."

"What's twenty minutes?"

"How long we lasted without arguing."

"We didn't fight. I was tempted, but being the mature woman I am, I managed to avoid telling you that I found that remark unnecessarily condescending."

Blake chuckled and took a sip of his wine. "I'm glad. Because then I can admit that sometimes I say things purposely just to see the anger spark in your eyes. You're beautiful when you let that invisible guard down, and sometimes anger is the only thing that lowers it."

Every part of her was conscious of Blake. Pressed close to his side, she ached for the urgent feel of his arms around her and the hungry taste of his mouth. But their truce wasn't limited to arguments, although they hadn't stated as much. They needed to find a level plain, a happy medium between the fighting and the loving.

"I'm working to change that about myself," Caasi admitted softly. "When Dad was in charge he was firm in his belief about mixing business with pleasure. When he was in the office he was one man and outside the office, another. In some ways I'm a lot like my father. We've worked together five years, Blake, but I never saw you as anything more than my general manager."

"And you do now?"

Her voice was becoming huskier as she strove to keep the emotion out of it. "Yes."

"Because I'm leaving?"

"Say . . ." She laughed shakily. "Why am I doing all the talking? Shouldn't you make some deep revelation about yourself?"

Blake's answering grin was dry. "I like fine wine"—he raised the glass to his lips and took a sip—"and the challenge of climbing mountains. I love the Pacific and enjoy walks along the beach in the early hours of the morning before the sun rises. Sometimes when the mood comes over me, I paint." He paused. "Does that satisfy your curiosity?"

"In some ways." But he didn't offer to reveal more, and the point was well noted.

The timer on the stove rang and Caasi reluctantly broke from his arms. "I'll check our dinner."

She set the quiche on top of the stove to cool and returned to the living room. Blake was looking out the window at the view.

"Some nights, especially when things are troubling me," Caasi admitted softly as she joined him, "I'll stand here and think."

"So that's why there's a worn spot in the carpet," Blake teased.

"I've been here frequently of late."

"Why?" Blake turned and took a step toward her. Only a few inches separated them.

Caasi lowered her gaze to the floor and shrugged. "Lots of things."

"Anything in particular?"

She ignored the question. "The quiche is ready if you are."

Blake brushed a strand of hair from her face. When his hand grazed her cheek, Caasi was forced to stifle an involuntary gasp of pleasure.

"No," Blake said slowly, his words barely audible. "I'm not ready." His hand worked its way around the back of her neck, his fingers twining into her hair as he brought her mouth up to meet his.

With a small cry of welcome, Caasi swayed into him, melting against him, her arms reaching instinctively for him. Her response was so automatic she didn't have time to question it.

As his mouth plundered hers, Caasi felt as though

she were on fire, the burning heat spreading down her legs until she was weak and clinging.

This wasn't supposed to happen, they'd promised one another it wouldn't, but they were like two climbers waiting to explore a mountain and would no longer be denied the thrill of the challenge.

When Blake's hand cupped her breast, her body throbbed with sensations that had been long denied. She didn't stop him when he unbuttoned her blouse, nor did he prevent her from pulling his shirt free from his pants.

Helping her off with her bra, Blake led Caasi to the sofa, his hands caressing the soft undersides of her breasts as his mouth made sensual, biting kisses at her lips.

Her roaming hands reveled in the feel of the hard muscles and smooth skin of his back. A delicious languor spread through her, and her breath came in sharp gasps.

Blake buried his face in the hollow of her throat and shuddered. "Let's eat," he whispered, and Caasi smiled at the husky timbre of his voice as she realized he was experiencing the same sensations she was.

When he sat up, Blake helped refasten her bra and blouse. Caasi needed the help; her fingers were trembling so hard she found the simple task awkward.

Neither showed much interest in the meal. Blake commented that she'd done a good job and Caasi was pleased with her efforts, but her mind wasn't on the food.

They hardly spoke, but each intuitively seemed to know what the other was thinking. Caasi wished she had her wine, and without a word Blake stood and brought it to her.

Simultaneously they set their forks across half-full plates, their interest in food entirely gone. Blake stood and held out his hand to her.

Heedless of where he was taking her, Caasi realized she would have followed him to Mars. She placed her hand in his. Blake inserted another tape into the player and led her back to the sofa.

Caasi slid an arm around him and rested the side of her face close to his heart. Blake rubbed his jaw against the top of her head in a slow, rotating action that was faintly hypnotic. His fingers were in her hair.

Caasi didn't need to look to know that his eyes were closed. This was like a dream, a trance from which she never wanted to wake. The barriers were down.

Caasi didn't know how long he held her. The music had faded long ago, but they made their own. Blake had made that comment to her when he'd given her the dancing lesson, but she hadn't understood him then. Now she didn't even need to close her eyes to hear the violins.

Blake shifted and Caasi was shocked to look at her watch and see that it was almost midnight.

"Walk me to the door," he whispered and kissed the crown of her head, his breath stirring her dark hair.

She nodded her agreement, not finding the words to release him readily.

"Our truce lasted," she said softly and added, with a warm smile, "sort of."

"If we're going to fight, let's do it like this.

Agreed?" He took her in his arms, gazing down at her upturned face with a warmth that reached all the way to her soul.

"Yes, I agree." Her hand lovingly stroked his thick, unruly hair. "Are you really going to leave me, Blake?"

He went completely still. "How do you mean?"

Did he think she was asking him to spend the night? If she was honest, she would admit the thought wasn't an alien one. But she had been sincere when she explained that she wasn't one to indulge in casual affairs. She wanted Blake; Caasi couldn't deny it. But she wanted him forever.

"The Empress," she explained. "You're not going to leave, are you?" The minute the words were out she knew she'd said the wrong thing.

Blake looked as if she'd physically struck him. Angrily he pulled her arms away, severing the contact. "So that was what this was all about." Hard impatience shadowed his face.

"Blake, no!" But he wasn't listening as he sharply turned, opened the door, and left.

"There's a Gina Sherrill to see you," Louise announced over the intercom the following Monday.

"Send her in," Caasi replied. "And, Louise, could you see to it that we're not disturbed?"

"Of course."

Gina stepped into the office a moment later.

"Hi, Caasi." She looked uncertain, her eyes taking in the expensive decor of the room. "Wow, you've got a great view from up here, haven't you? How do you ever get anything done?"

"It's hard, especially on a sunny day like today when it seems that the whole world is outside this window and ready to be explored."

"We missed you Sunday."

Caasi rolled a pencil between her palms. "I had a previous engagement." The lie was only a small one.

"Everyone likes you, and we were hoping you'd come again."

"I will," Caasi assured her but secretly doubted that she could. Not with Blake in his present state of mind. Another confrontation with him was to be avoided at all costs. They treated one another like polite strangers. Blake had hired his replacement and was training the middle-aged man now. Caasi liked Brian Harris and had recognized almost instantly that she wouldn't have any trouble working with him.

Blake's last day was scheduled for the end of the month, less than ten days away.

"Let's go down to the Blue Room and you can tell me what kind of decorations you want. Are the other women coming?" Caasi asked. Gina had asked to include her maid of honor and bridesmaids in the shower planning.

"They're in the lobby. We didn't feel like we should all descend on you."

"Why not?" Caasi asked, setting the pencil aside. "I'm looking forward to meeting them."

"Blake's leaving, isn't he?" Gina's question came as a surprise.

Caasi nodded with forced calm. "Yes; he handed in his resignation not long ago."

"I'm surprised." Gina wrinkled her nose. "I didn't think Blake would ever leave you."

That was the crux of the problem—Caasi hadn't thought so either.

"Shall we go now?" Caasi wanted to divert the conversation from Blake.

"Sure," Gina answered eagerly.

Riding the elevator down to the lobby Gina announced, "All the invitations have been mailed. Everyone is impressed that the shower's at the Empress. I'm still having problems believing it myself."

"I'm glad to do it." Caasi meant that.

"You'll be there, won't you? I know it's in the middle of the day and everything, but you wouldn't have to stay long and I'd really like everyone to meet you."

Caasi hesitated. There was an important meeting scheduled with some architects the afternoon of the shower, and if past experience was anything to go by, she could be held up for hours.

"I won't make any promises, but I'll see what I can do."

"Great," Gina enthused.

They met the others in the lobby, and the small party took the broad, winding stairs built against a mirrored wall to the second floor where the Blue Room was situated.

"Oh." Gina sighed with excitement. "It's perfect, just perfect."

Caasi stayed only a few minutes longer. She wanted to have some time to herself before she had to leave for a luncheon engagement that was scheduled with the Portland Chamber of Commerce; they would be discussing plans for a basketball players' convention that winter.

THE TROUBLE WITH CAASI

Briefly Caasi explained to Gina that she'd ordered the flowers delivered Thursday morning and had asked the chef to provide a sketch of the cake.

"The cake," Gina said happily, "is larger than the one for the wedding."

Glancing at her wristwatch, Caasi sighed. "I've got to run, but I'll see you Thursday afternoon."

"Oh, thanks, Caasi. I can't tell you how excited I am about this."

"To be honest, I'm having as much fun as you, doing it."

Caasi took the elevator back to her office. As the huge doors glided open, Caasi stepped into the wide hallway—and nearly bumped into Blake.

His hands shot out to help her maintain her balance and their eyes clashed. "Are you all right?"

Caasi couldn't take her eyes from his face. For the first time in days there was a faint flicker of something more than polite disregard. Every angle of the harsh jaw was lovingly familiar, and she longed to ease the lines of strain from his eyes and mouth.

"Caasi," he said sharply.

Her eyes studied the floor, and she struggled to maintain the thin thread of her composure. "I'm fine."

He released her slowly. "Will you have time this afternoon to go over the Wilson figures?"

"Yes, that shouldn't be any problem. I'll be back around two."

"Fine," he said in clipped tones. "I'll send Harris into your office then."

"Harris." She repeated the name. She knew the man was replacing Blake, but she had yet to deal with him directly. "Yes." Her voice faltered a bit. "That'll be fine."

Caasi stepped into her office and retrieved her purse. "I'm leaving now."

Louise looked up at her blankly. The luncheon wasn't scheduled for another hour. "But Mr. Gains is due to see you in twenty minutes."

"Send him in to Blake," Caasi said curtly. "You know where to reach him."

Caasi took the Mercedes, heading east down Sandy Boulevard until she located Broadway. She drove around for several fruitless minutes. It had to be around here somewhere. Finally she recalled seeing that small mom-and-pop grocery and knew she was headed in the right direction. For all her years in Portland, she'd been to Rocky Butte only once. With Blake, the night of his cousin's wedding.

She parked her car in the same area Blake had. The scene was all the more magnificent during the day. The snow-capped mountain peaks of the Cascade range, the flowing Columbia and Willamette rivers, could all be seen from there. Washington State was just on the other side of the Columbia River Gorge, and powerful Mount St. Helens was in full view. No wonder Blake loved it up there so much.

The park itself was a different matter. Someone had broken beer bottles against the steps, and Caasi avoided the sharp pieces of glass as she climbed the flights of rock-hewn stairs for the second time. Walking to the parapet, she studied the view again. Faint

THE TROUBLE WITH CAASI 101

stirrings of love and appreciation for what lay before her brought an involuntary smile. Caasi, born and raised in Portland, Oregon, was unaware of her city's charm and beauty. A shame, she mused dejectedly.

Caasi sauntered into the office a little after two, having decided to send Harris to the luncheon. Louise glanced up at her nervously.

"Mr. Sherrill's in your office."

"Thanks, Louise." Her secretary's tone told her Blake wasn't in a mood to exchange pleasantries.

"Problems, Blake?" she quizzed as she entered.

He swiveled and jammed his hands into his pockets. His gaze hardened angrily. "Gains had the appointment with you. Where were you?"

"Out," she snapped.

"You don't give important people like Gains the brush-off like that. The banker was furious, and with good reason."

Perfectly calm, Caasi sat at her desk and glared at him. "Do you presume to tell me how to run Crane Enterprises now? Criticizing my personal life isn't enough?"

Blake clamped his mouth closed. "You're in no mood to discuss this rationally."

Caasi's laugh was sarcastic and brittle. "This is getting better every minute." She took a cigarette out of the top drawer and lit it. The lighter's flame curled over the tip of the cigarette. "Send Harry in with the Wilson figures, please." She inhaled once and put the cigarette out, not liking the taste it left in her dry mouth.

"The man's name is Harris." The contempt in Blake's eyes was enough to make her cry. Maybe tears would dissolve the lump of loneliness within her. Maybe tears would take away the pain of what Blake was doing. But somehow Caasi doubted it.

Thursday afternoon, fifteen minutes before her scheduled meeting with the architects, Caasi took the elevator to the Blue Room, where Gina's wedding shower was in progress.

She stood in the entry watching the young girl open her gifts. The turnout was a good one, and Caasi recognized several people from Kathleen's wedding.

The bouquets of blue and white flowers harmonized beautifully with the room's decor. The chef had outdone himself with the huge sheet cake.

Gina saw Caasi just inside the doorway and gave a squeal of delight. The young bride-to-be hurried to proudly introduce Caasi to her friends.

Caasi's appearance was only a token one, and she made her farewells, sorry to learn that she'd missed Anne. She would have enjoyed seeing Blake's mother again.

Louise smiled when Caasi returned to the office. "There was a Mrs. Sherrill here to see you. I told her you'd gone down to the Blue Room."

Caasi smiled sadly. She'd just missed Anne again. But that was the way her life was headed. Always close but never close enough.

She'd barely sat down at her desk when Blake slammed into her office, nearly taking her door off the hinges when he closed it.

"What was my mother doing here?" he demanded.

"Your mother was here because of Gina's shower," Caasi replied calmly.

"Gina's wedding shower?" He was pacing the floor like a caged lion eager for the opportunity to escape and hunt the closest victim.

"Yes. It's in the Blue Room."

"My family can't afford the Blue Room."

"But I can. I'm doing this for Gina."

Blake froze, and his anger burned from every pore. "You did what?"

"I would have said something earlier if we'd been on better terms. Everything I do lately angers you. There are only a few days left until you're free of me. Must you fight me at every turn?"

Blake marched to the far side of the office and raked his hand through his hair. "I want you to add up every cent that this fiasco has cost and take it out of my next paycheck."

"What?" Caasi exploded, bolting out of her chair.

"You heard me. Every cent."

Hot tears sprang into her eyes, blinding her. She lowered her gaze so Blake wouldn't notice.

"Why?" she asked, amazed that her voice could remain so steady when she felt as though the world was crumbling apart beneath her.

"I told you before that you couldn't buy yourself a family. Least of all mine."

"Yes, of course." She swallowed at the painful hoarseness in her throat. "Now, if you'll excuse me."

She nearly walked into Louise. "Conference Room A is ready for . . ." Louise stopped sharply. "Miss

Crane, are you all right? Do you need a doctor?" The woman looked flabbergasted to see Caasi in tears. Hurriedly she supplied Caasi with a tissue.

"Cancel the meeting, Louise." Her voice trembling, Caasi fought down a sob. "Please extend my sincere apologies." With as much self-possession as she could muster, Caasi walked out of the office.

Blake came up behind her. "Caasi." Her name was issued grimly.

She ignored him and stepped into the elevator. When she turned around their eyes met. The tall, lean figure swam in and out of her vision.

"You have so much, Blake. Is it that difficult to share just this little bit with me?" The huge metal doors swished shut and Caasi broke into sobs that heaved her shoulders and shook her whole body.

Chapter Six

Caasi leaned against the penthouse door, her face buried in her hands as her shoulders shook. If this horrible ache was part of being a woman, she wanted none of it. Ink in her veins was preferable to the pain in her heart. But it was too late and Caasi recognized that.

Arms hugging her stomach, she tilted her face to the ceiling to keep the tears from spilling. She was tired. The weariness came from deep within.

Blake was leaving; why shouldn't she? She hadn't been on a real vacation in years, not since she took over Crane Enterprises.

Wiping the moisture from her cheeks, she took a quivering breath and stood at her favorite place by the window. She'd be fine. All she needed was a few days away to gain perspective.

Her leather luggage was stored in the bedroom closet. Caasi wasn't exactly sure where she'd go. It would be fun just to drive down the coast. Oregon had some of the most beautiful coastline in the world.

The soft knock on the door surprised her. Probably Louise. The secretary had been shocked to see Caasi cry . . . and little wonder. Caasi wasn't the weeping female type.

"Yes," Caasi called softly, striving to sound composed and confident. "Come in."

When Blake strolled into the living room, Caasi felt ice form in the pit of her stomach. "These are my private quarters," she told him in a voice that was dipped in acid. "I don't know who or what has given you the impression that you may come up here, but that has got to change. Now, get out before I call Security." She marched out of the room and into her bedroom, carelessly tossing her clothes into the suitcase.

"Caasi, listen." There was an unfamiliar pleading quality to his voice as he followed her. "Let me apologize."

"Okay," she said without looking up. "You're sorry. Now leave."

"What are you doing?" His eyes followed her as she moved from the closet to the suitcase, then back to the closet.

"That's none of your business."

"Like hell! If you're going someplace, I need to know."

"I'll leave the details of my trip with Louise." She didn't look at him; she was having enough trouble just keeping her composure intact.

"Isn't this trip a bit sudden?"

"Since when do you have the authority to question me?" She whirled around, placing her hands challengingly on slim hips.

"Since you started acting like an irrational female," he returned sarcastically.

"Me?" Caasi exploded. "Of all the nerve!" She stormed across the room and picked up the phone. "Security, please."

"I'm not leaving," Blake threatened. "Call out the National Guard, but I'm not leaving until we understand one another."

"Understand?" Caasi cried. "What's there to understand? I'm the boss, you're the employee. Now get out."

"No."

"Yes." Caasi spoke into the receiver. "This is Miss Crane. I'm having a problem here. Could you send up one of the security men?" She hung up the phone and tossed Blake a hard look. "Oh, before I forget," she said and gave him a saccharin smile, "be sure and have accounting give you an employee discount on the Blue Room." She slammed the lid of her suitcase closed and dragged it off the top of the bed.

Taking a smaller case, she entered the master bathroom and impatiently stuffed brush, comb, shampoo, hair dryer, and an entire cupboard of cosmetics into it. When she whirled around, Blake was blocking the doorway.

"Will you kindly step out of the way?"

"Not until we talk."

Expelling a long sigh to give the impression of boredom, Caasi crossed her arms and glared at him.

"All right, you win. Say what you want to say and be done with it."

Blake looked surprised but determined. He paused and ran his hand over his jaw.

"What's the matter, has the cat got your tongue?" she taunted unfairly.

Confusion flickered across his brow. "There's something about you, Caasi, that makes me say and do things I know are going to hurt you. Yet I do them."

"This is supposed to be an apology?" She faked a yawn.

Blake's thick brows drew together in a pained, confused expression. Caasi doubted that her feigned indifference could create a fissure in the hard wall of his defenses.

The phone rang, diverting her attention to the other room.

"If you'll excuse me."

"No, not now." His arm across the door prevented her from leaving.

"Blake." She groaned in frustration. "This is ridiculous; look at you. Now, for heaven's sake, will you let me out of the bathroom so I can answer the phone?"

He didn't budge.

"Please," she added.

Blake dropped his hand and turned his back to her. As she hurried past him, Caasi noted fleetingly that he looked as weary and defeated as she felt.

"Hello," she answered on the fourth ring, her voice slightly breathless.

"Caasi?" The male voice on the other end was only faintly recognizable.

"Burt?" Caasi felt all the blood drain from her face.

"It's June. She's in labor. She said I should phone you now."

"Now?" Caasi repeated with a sense of unreality. "Isn't this early?"

"Only ten days. The doctor assured us it wasn't anything to worry about. I'm at the hospital; the nurse is checking June and said she'd prefer I stepped out for a few minutes." Burt sounded worried and unsure.

"I'll be there in five minutes." Caasi's heart was singing with excitement as she replaced the telephone receiver.

"Who was it?"

Caasi had forgotten Blake was there. "Burt. June's in labor." She grabbed her purse from the end of the bed and hurried out of the suite. A security man met her just outside the door.

"You wanted me, Miss Crane?"

"Yes," she shouted and shot past him to the elevator. "I mean, no, everything's been taken care of. I'm sorry to have troubled you."

"No trouble, miss." He touched the brim of his hat with his index finger.

"Caasi," Blake called as he followed her out of the suite. "I'll meet with the architects and we can talk about it in the morning."

"Fine." She'd have agreed to anything as long as it didn't delay her.

The car engine roared to life when she turned the

key. Caasi wondered if June was experiencing this same kind of exhilarated excitement. Burt and June wanted this baby so much and had planned carefully for it. For *her,* Caasi corrected her thoughts. June's deepest desire was for a little girl.

The visitors' parking lot was full, and Caasi spent several frustrating minutes until she found a space on the street. On her visit the previous Friday, she had learned that once Burt phoned she was to go directly to the labor room on the third floor. Stepping off the elevator, her shoes clapped against the polished, squeaky-clean floor.

"I'm Caasi Crane," she announced at the nurses' station. "Can you tell me which labor room Mrs. Kauffman is in?"

The uniformed nurse with white hair and a wide smile glanced at the chart. "Number 304. I believe her husband is with her."

"Thanks," Caasi said with a smile.

The room was the second one on the left side of the hall. The door was closed, so Caasi knocked lightly.

Burt opened it for her, looking pale and worried.

"Is anything wrong?" Caasi asked anxiously.

"No, everything's fine." He ran his hand through his hair. "June's doing great."

Caasi smiled. "How come you look like *you're* the one in labor?"

"I don't know, Caasi, I can hardly stand to see June in pain like this."

"Caasi?" June looked flushed against the white sheets. "Is that you?"

"I'm here."

"I suppose I got you out of some important meeting."

"Nothing I wasn't glad to escape from," Caasi assured her and pulled up a chair so she could sit beside the bed. "I've read that babies aren't particularly known for their sense of timing."

June laughed weakly. "At least not this one. The pains woke me up this morning, but I wasn't really sure this was the real thing. I didn't want to trouble you if it wasn't."

Burt came around to the other side of the bed and took his wife's hand in both of his. "How do you feel?" His eyes were filled with such tenderness that it hurt Caasi to look at him. Would any man ever look at her like that? The only thing she'd seen in Blake's eyes lately was disdain.

"I'm fine, so quit worrying about me. Women have been having babies since the beginning of time."

Burt looked up at Caasi. "I'll say one thing; having a baby is a lot different than I thought."

Caasi smiled reassuringly. "I don't imagine it's much what June thought either." She glanced down to note that June's face was twisted with pain. Instinctively, Caasi gave June her hand. Her friend gripped it the way a drowning man would a life preserver. The young face relaxed.

"The pains last about thirty seconds, but it's the longest thirty seconds of my life," June whispered.

"The last time the nurse checked, she'd dilated to five centimeters. She has to get to ten centimeters in the first stage of labor."

Caasi had been reading the book the doctor had

given her in preparation for the big event. Once June was fully dilated, the second stage of labor, when the baby entered the birth canal, would begin.

"The nurse said that won't be for hours yet," June told her.

"Not to worry, I've got all day. What about you?"

"Well, if the truth be known, I'm missing a big sale at Lloyd Center," June admitted with a weak smile.

The hours passed quickly. Caasi was shocked to look up from timing a contraction to note that it was after seven, and she hadn't eaten lunch. But she was too busy to care about food.

When the hard contractions came, Burt coached his wife, while Caasi, her hand on June's abdomen, counted out the seconds. Time and again Caasi was astonished at her friend's fortitude. June and Burt had decided in the beginning that they wanted natural childbirth, and although the pains were excruciating, June's resolve didn't waver. Burt didn't look as confident.

When the time came to move into the delivery room, Caasi and Burt were asked to don surgical gowns.

"I didn't realize I would have to dress for the occasion," Caasi joked as June reached for her hand.

A small cry slipped from June as the pain crescendoed. As it ebbed, June lay back on the pillow, panting.

Burt carried June's fingers to his lips. Then, tenderly, he wiped the moisture from her brow.

"I love you," June whispered, the soft light of love shining in her eyes.

Strangely, Caasi didn't feel like an intruder on the

touching scene; she felt she was a part of it—a wonderful, important part.

"I've never loved you more than I do right this minute," Burt whispered in return.

Another pain came and June bit into her lip with the grinding agony, panting and breathless when it waned.

"One more pain and you should be able to see the head," the doctor told them. A round mirror was positioned near the ceiling, and all eyes focused on the reflection as another pain came and passed. June gave Caasi a happy but weak smile.

The baby started crying once the head was free of the birth canal, the doctor supporting the tiny skull.

"Good pair of lungs," Burt said excitedly. "It must be a girl."

One final contraction and the baby slipped into the doctor's waiting hands.

"It's a girl," he announced.

June gave an exhilarated cry. "Oh, I wanted a girl so badly. Burt . . . a girl." Laughing and crying at the same time, she threw her arms around her husband's neck, hugging him fiercely.

"Seven pounds, twelve ounces," the nurse said as she lifted the squalling baby from the scale.

Unabashed tears of happiness flowed down Caasi's cheeks. She had never felt such wondrous joy in her life. To have had even a small part in the baby's birth produced warm emotions that touched the softest core of her heart.

"Caasi." June gripped her hand. "You're crying. I don't think I've ever seen you cry."

"It's all so beautiful. And your daughter's beautiful."

"Should I tell her?" Burt looked down with love at his wife. At June's confirming nod, he glanced up. "June and I decided if we had a daughter we would name her Cassi—two *s*'s, one *a*."

"After a lifelong friend we both love and respect," June added.

Caasi couldn't push the words of love and appreciation past the lump of happiness in her throat.

"And, of course, we want you to be her godmother," Burt continued.

"Of course," Caasi confirmed, tears winding a crooked path down her face.

An hour later, Caasi walked to her car parked on the deserted street. A look at her watch confirmed that it was almost ten. She felt like skipping and singing. Tiny, sweet baby Cassi was adorable, and Caasi couldn't love her any more if she were her own.

Caasi pulled onto the avenue and merged with the flow of traffic. She felt wonderful and rolled down the window, singing as she cheerfully missed the turn that would lead her back to the downtown area and the Empress.

Before she could reconsider, she took the turnoff for Gresham and Blake's house. He'd said something about wanting to talk to her after the meeting that afternoon, but that wasn't the reason she had to see him. If she didn't tell someone about the baby, she'd burst.

There wasn't a streetlight to guide her as she drove down the winding road. She had to pull over to the side of the road a couple of times, having difficulty finding her way in the night. Finally she pulled into the driveway, the old weeping willow the only reminder she required.

The kitchen lights were on, and Caasi paused before climbing out of the car and slowly closing the door. Maybe coming to Blake's wasn't such a good idea after all. They'd been fighting when she left.

The back door opened and Blake came down the steps. "Caasi." He sounded shocked. "Is anything wrong?"

She shook her head. "June had a baby girl."

"That's wonderful. Come inside and I'll make you a cup of coffee."

"I'd like that."

A hand at her elbow guided her up the stairs. The coffeepot was on the stove. Caasi glanced into the living room and saw an open book lying across the arm of an overstuffed chair. Blake had been spending a quiet evening at home reading.

He handed her a mug and Caasi took it, leaning against the kitchen counter as she hugged the coffee cup with both hands.

"June and Burt are naming her Cassi—two *s*'s, one *a*. She's so beautiful, all pink and with the tiniest hands. She's perfect, just perfect. Before they moved her out of the delivery room, the nurse let me hold her for a few minutes. It was the most incredibly marvelous thing I've ever experienced, holding this new life. I still can't believe it," she finished breathlessly.

A warm smile appeared on his face and was reflected in his eyes as he watched her. "Come and sit down in the living room. You can tell me all about it."

"I don't even know where to start." She sat in the chair opposite his and lifted the lid from a candy jar nearby, popping a couple of pieces of hard candy into her mouth. "I'm starved. I hope you don't mind if I help myself."

"Didn't you eat dinner?"

Caasi shook her head. "Not lunch either. No time," she explained while sucking the lemon drops. The sugary sweetness filled her mouth, making her hunger more pronounced.

"Let me fix you something."

"No, I'll be fine, really," she asserted.

Blake ignored her, returning to the kitchen and opening the refrigerator as Caasi trailed after him. "There are leftover pork chops, eggs, bacon. What's your pleasure?"

Caasi bit into the side of her mouth to keep from saying: *You.* The thought nearly squeezed the oxygen from her lungs. Never had she wanted a home and husband more than she did at that moment. They even looked like an old married couple, standing in the kitchen, roaming through the fridge and looking for leftovers.

"Caasi?" Blake glanced up, his look questioning.

She shook her head. "Anything's fine. Don't worry about a meal, a sandwich would do as well."

"Bacon and eggs," he decided for her, taking both from the refrigerator and setting them on top of the counter.

Caasi pulled out a chair and sat at the table while Blake peeled off thick slices of bacon and laid them across a skillet.

"June was marvelous," Caasi continued. "She was a real trooper. Burt and June had decided they wanted natural childbirth and she didn't waver, not once. The doctor tried to encourage her to use the anesthesiologist a couple of times—it would have made his job easier. But June refused." She paused and smiled. "It's a good thing the doctor didn't ask Burt. He could barely stand to see June suffer. Instead of watching, he closed his eyes along with her. Don't get me wrong; he was wonderful too. I don't know how any woman can have a baby without her husband's help. I know I couldn't." Caasi swallowed tightly. But then, she probably wouldn't have a child. Some of the enthusiasm left her and she stared into the coffee mug.

A disturbing silence filled the kitchen.

"The meeting with Schultz and Son went fine. But they'd like you to make a trip to Seaside next Tuesday, if you can."

"I don't see why not." Eagerly Caasi picked up the conversation. "I don't remember that anything's scheduled. I'll check with Louise in the morning." Her index finger made a lazy circle on the tabletop. "Will you be coming?" Blake sometimes traveled with her, depending on the circumstances.

"It looks as if I'll have to. We'll leave Harris in the office, which will be good experience for him."

"Sure," she agreed, feeling somewhat guilty. Not once in the past week had she made an effort to meet or talk to Brian Harris. The man only served to remind her that Blake was leaving, and she hadn't accepted that. *Couldn't* accept it. Not yet.

The bacon grease was sizzling in the frying pan when Blake cracked two eggs against the side and let them slide into the hot fat. With the dexterity of an accomplished chef he flipped down the toaster switch.

"Hey, I didn't realize you were that skilled in the kitchen," Caasi murmured, uneasy with the fact that he could cook and she couldn't.

"Practice makes perfect, and I've cooked plenty of solitary meals in my time," he said as he slid the fried eggs onto a plate. He set the meal in front of her and straddled a chair, drinking his coffee while she ate.

Everything was delicious and she said as much. "I don't remember a time I've enjoyed a meal more." At his skeptical look, Caasi laughed and crossed her heart with her finger. "Honest."

"Then I suggest you have a talk with that expensive chef you imported."

Blake had never approved of her hiring the Frenchman who ran the Empress kitchen.

"I'd be willing to do away with the whole kitchen staff if you'd agree to stay."

Forcefully Blake expelled his breath, and Caasi realized that she'd done it again.

Lowering her gaze to the empty plate, she tore a piece of crust from her toast. "That was a dumb joke. I didn't mean it." For once, just tonight, when she was so happy, she didn't want to say or do anything that would start a disagreement.

"Didn't you?" he asked in a low, troubled voice.

Caasi peered at him through thick lashes. "Well, it's true I don't want you to go, but my reasons are entirely selfish."

"You don't need me anymore."

Dear Lord, if only he knew. "I guess not," she agreed reluctantly, "but you've always been there, and it won't be the same when you're gone."

"Sure it will."

How could he sound so casual about leaving the place that had been his second home for eight years? Did she mean so little to him? Instead of seeking answers to the nagging doubts, Caasi scooted out of her chair and stood.

"I'll do the dishes. Anyone who does the cooking shouldn't have to do the dishes."

"Caasi Crane doing dishes," Blake said mockingly. "This I've got to see."

"Well, just who do you think did them the night we baked the quiche?" she declared righteously. "I am a capable person, Blake, whether you care to admit it or not."

She washed while he dried and put away. Wordlessly they worked together, but it wasn't a strained silence.

When they finished, Caasi noted that it was very late . . . they both had to be at work in the morning. There wasn't any reason to stay, but she didn't want to go.

"I suppose I should think about heading back," she murmured as she dried her hands on a kitchen towel.

Blake agreed with a curt nod, but he didn't look as though he wanted her to leave either.

Caasi glanced at the oil painting over the fireplace. "Have you done any art work lately?" Maybe some small talk would delay her departure.

"Not much to speak of." He shrugged his shoulders. "I'm thinking about concentrating more on my painting after the first of the month."

After the first—when he would no longer be at the Empress and wouldn't be troubled with her anymore.

"Let me know; I'd like to buy something from you."

Blake laughed outright. "I only dabble in art. The Empress displays paintings from some of the best in the country. Those artists would be insulted to have my work hanging beside theirs."

Caasi hadn't been thinking of hanging it in the hotel, but in her suite. It would give her something tangible to remember him by. But rather than admit it, she said nothing.

"We did it," Caasi murmured as they strolled toward her car.

"Did what?"

"Went the whole night, or at least a portion of it, without fighting. That's a record, I think."

"You mentioned my resignation only once."

"I won't admit how many times I've had to bite my tongue," Caasi teased.

"Is my leaving that difficult for you to accept?" Blake leaned against the front of her car and folded his arms across his chest.

Caasi shrugged both delicate shoulders. "Yes," she admitted starkly. "But I'm beginning to understand how selfish I'm being toward you. There's something about having you with me . . . I trust you, Blake—sometimes more than I do myself. Looking back, I can see the mistakes I've made in my enthusiasm to live up to Dad's expectations. I allowed Crane Enterprises to become my life."

For a long second he looked at her. "But not anymore?"

"I don't know," she admitted honestly. "But I'd do anything if you'd change your mind."

Indecision flickered in his narrowed gaze. "You're handing me a powerful weapon; you know that, don't you, Caasi?"

"You're worth it."

"To Crane Enterprises?"

She nodded. "And me," she told him softly.

He was silent for so long that Caasi wasn't sure if he'd heard her.

"Let me think about it," Blake said. Looking away, he took a deep breath, as if struggling within himself.

"How soon before you can give me an answer?" Her heart was beating double time. If Blake stayed she would have the opportunity to explore the relationship that was developing between them. The thought of losing him now—just when she was discovering Blake, the man—was intolerable.

"I'll let you know by the first of the week."

"Great," Caasi agreed. At least there was a chance.

Chapter Seven

Monday morning Caasi strolled into the outer office and greeted her secretary with a cheerful, "Good morning."

Louise glanced up. A frown drove deep grooves into her wide brow. "Good morning, Miss Crane."

Caasi was sure Louise didn't know what to think of her anymore. Her secretary probably attributed the wide swings in her moods to Blake's resignation. Not immune to office gossip, Caasi was aware that there was heavy speculation as to his reasons.

Today she would know his decision. How could he refuse her after all that they'd shared recently? How could he walk away from her on a day as gorgeous and sunny as this one? He wouldn't, Caasi was sure of it.

In her office, she buzzed the intercom. "Louise,

would you ask Mr. Sherrill to come to my office when he arrives?"

"I think he's in now."

"Good."

Caasi released the switch and sauntered to the far side of the room. So much had changed between her and Blake in such a short time. Mostly there was Blake to thank for that. And he'd see that she was changing and that would be all the incentive he'd need to stay.

Friday she'd watched him, studied his body language as well as his speech. He didn't want to leave, she was sure of it. Her father had warned her of the hazards of being overconfident, but she didn't feel the necessity to heed his counsel this morning. Not this glorious morning.

Caasi had spent Sunday with June, Burt, and baby Cassi. June had come home from the hospital, and while Burt had fussed over his wife, Caasi had sat and held the baby. Cradling the tiny being in her arms had filled her heart with love. This was what it meant to be a woman, whole and complete. The overwhelming tenderness she'd experienced holding the baby lingered even now, a day later.

Sunday night Caasi had lain awake staring at the ceiling, unable to sleep. So much depended on Blake's decision. Her father had taught her to hope for the best but plan for the worst. What would change if Blake decided to leave? Ultimately nothing. Brian Harris seemed capable enough of assuming Blake's duties. But losing Blake the man would be more than Caasi could bear. Not now, not when she was just coming into her own. Surely he'd see the changes in her and withdraw his resignation.

"Good morning," Blake said as he entered the room. "You wanted to see me?"

"Yes." Caasi nodded, standing at her desk. One look at Blake and a nauseous feeling attacked her stomach. He looked terrible. "Blake, are you ill?"

"No," he denied with an abrupt shake of his head. "I suspect you want to hear my decision."

"Of course I do," she said somewhat sharply. What she wanted to do was scream at him to say what she needed to hear: the promise that he'd never leave her, that he'd stay with her all her life.

Blake rubbed a hand over his eyes. "This decision hasn't been easy," he said softly.

"I know," she whispered in return. *Dear God,* her mind screamed, *don't let him leave me.*

"I can't stay, Cupcake."

Caasi slumped into her chair, fighting to disguise the effect of his decision by squaring her shoulders and clamping her hands together in her lap. "Why?"

Blake lowered himself into the chair on the other side of her desk. "Not for the same reasons I originally resigned," he explained.

"I see," Caasi replied stiffly. "In other words—"

"In other words," Blake interrupted, "things have changed between us."

"For the better," she inserted, not easily dissuaded. "I've tried so hard."

"Too hard, Cupcake."

Caasi couldn't respond as the continued waves of hurt and shock rippled over her.

"In light of my decision, maybe it would be best if Brian Harris accompanied you tomorrow."

Somehow, with a determined effort, Caasi managed to nod.

"My last day is Wednesday, but if you think you'd like me to stay a few more days . . ."

"No." She nearly shouted the word. "No," she repeated softly. "If you've made your decision, then don't prolong the inevitable."

"You're beginning to sound like your father again."

"Again?" Caasi asked with a dry smile. "I've always sounded like Dad. Why shouldn't I? After all, I am his daughter."

"Caasi . . ." Blake sounded unsure.

"If you'll excuse me, I've got a meeting to attend." She spoke crisply and centered her gaze just past him on the seascape hanging on the wall.

The door clicked and Caasi realized that Blake had left. Taking deep breaths helped to calm her pounding heart. She was stunned, completely and totally shocked.

"Louise." Her hand was surprisingly steady as she held down the intercom switch. "Do I have anything pressing this morning?"

Her secretary ran down a list of appointments.

"Would you reschedule them at a more convenient time, please? I'm going out for awhile."

"Going out?" Louise repeated disbelievingly. "But there's the meeting with Jefferson at nine."

"I'll be here for that, but cancel everything else."

"The whole day?"

"No." Caasi pressed a hand to her forehead. She

was overreacting. She had to come to grips with herself. "Just this morning."

An hour later Caasi couldn't have repeated one word of the meeting with Jefferson. The accountant seemed to be aware of her lack of attention and called their time short. Caasi didn't return to her office but went directly to the parking garage and took out her Mercedes.

The drive to the Lloyd Center was accomplished in only a matter of minutes. Leaving her car in the underground parking garage, she took the escalator to the second-floor shopping level. Standing at the rail, she looked down at the ice-skating rink situated in the middle of the huge complex.

A sad smile touched her eyes as she watched the figures circle the silvery ice. Most of the skaters were senior citizens, loving couples with their arms around one another as they skillfully glided around the rink. Thirty years from now she could picture June and Burt skating like that. Thirty years from now and she would remain an observer, standing on the outside of life—exactly as she was now.

In the mood to spend money, Caasi went from store to store, buying whatever took her fancy. She bought baby Cassi enough clothes to see her into grade school. She also bought toys, blankets, shoes—whatever attracted her attention. Caasi held up one frilly outfit after another and understood why June had wanted a baby girl.

Returning to the hotel garage, she left instructions for the packages to be taken to her quarters. The last thing she needed was for Blake to see what she'd bought and accuse her of buying herself another family.

Louise glanced up and smiled when Caasi stepped into the outer office.

"Happy Monday," Caasi said and handed her secretary a small box.

"What's this for?" Louise pulled the gold elastic ribbon off the box.

"Just a thank you for rearranging the day."

Her announcement was followed by a short gasp of pleasure from Louise. "Chocolates from How Sweet It Is. But they're twenty dollars a pound."

"You deserve only the best."

For the first time in years, Louise looked completely flustered. "Thank you, Miss Crane."

"Thank *you*, Louise," Caasi stated sincerely.

The stack of phone messages was thick. Caasi shuffled through them and paused at the one from Dirk Evans from The International Hotel chain. He'd phoned several times in the past few years, eager to talk to her about acquiring the Empress. International was interested not only in the Portland Empress but also in several others in California and along the Oregon coast.

She stared at the pink slip for several moments while pacing the floor. Pausing at the window, she examined her options. Her father would turn over in his grave if she were to sell. But why did she need the hotels? Why did she need any of this? Even without the hotels she was a wealthy woman. No, the thought of unburdening herself was tempting at the moment, but the Empress was her family, the only family she'd ever known, the only family she would ever know. She couldn't throw that away, not on a whim.

Louise buzzed and broke into her thoughts. "Call from Edie Albright on line one."

"Thanks, Louise." Caasi released one button and pushed down another. "Edie, how are you?"

"Fine."

"You don't sound fine. What's wrong?"

"Fredd's in New York and I'm bored. I don't suppose you'd be interested in dinner with me tonight? Nothing fancy. I could come to the Empress if you'd like."

"I'd like it very much. I'm feeling a little down myself." That was a gross understatement, but if she admitted as much they'd both be crying in their salads.

"Great." Edie cheered up immediately. "What time?"

"Any time you like."

Edie paused. "My goodness, you're accommodating today. I expected an argument at the very least. You don't go out that often."

Caasi smiled drily. "And how would you know that?"

"Honestly, Caasi, June and I are your best friends. We know you."

"Apparently not well enough," Caasi couldn't resist adding. "I'll meet you at seven in the main dining room."

"Wonderful. You don't know how much I appreciate this," Edie said with sigh. "I've got lots to tell you. This pregnancy stuff isn't all it's cracked up to be."

Caasi replaced the receiver a few minutes later and

stared into space a while longer. Seeing Edie that night was just what she needed. Her friend, scheming and crazy, had a refreshing way of helping her see the bright side of things. And she'd need a lot of talking to see the pot of gold at the end of the rainbow as far as Blake's leaving was concerned.

The afternoon passed in a whirl of appointments and phone calls. By six Louise had left, and although there were several items on Caasi's desk that needed her immediate attention, she decided to deal with them Wednesday. The next day she'd be flying to Seaside with Brian Harris to meet with the architects. The time spent with Harris would help her become acquainted with the man. They'd be working closely in the future, and there was no reason to delay knowing one another. *No reason,* her mind repeated, and a curious pain attacked her heart.

Wednesday would be Blake's last day. As she pushed the elevator button, Caasi wondered how or where she would get the courage to relinquish him as unemotionally as possible.

Her living room was filled with packages from that morning's shopping spree. Caasi decided to ignore them until after her bath. She didn't want to keep Edie waiting.

The bath water was running when there was an abrupt knock on her door.

Caasi wasn't sure it was someone at her door until the sound was repeated. "Just a minute," she called and hurried to turn off the water. She was grateful that she hadn't completely undressed. Grabbing a housecoat, she tied the sash as she walked across the living room carpet.

"I thought I said seven in the dining room," Caasi murmured good-naturedly as she opened the door. Her jaw must have sagged.

"Can I come in?" Blake looked at her, his eyes sparkling with amusement as he surveyed her appearance.

"I . . . I'm not dressed for visitors," Caasi stammered, her heart pounding wildly.

"Get dressed then, if it'll make you feel more comfortable."

Numbly, she stepped aside, swinging open the door.

"I'll only take a minute of your time," Blake promised with a half smile.

"I think I'd prefer to be dressed even if it is only for a minute," she said. Why had he come? She wasn't ready to deal with him. Not that night, not after he'd announced his decision. "If you'll excuse me." She turned around and nearly choked. The packages from her shopping spree covered the sofa and chair. She closed her eyes and groaned inwardly. The only thing she could do was ignore them now. If she called Blake's attention to the parcels and boxes that covered the sofa it would only invite comment.

Her fingers shook as she hurriedly donned her blouse, fumbling with the tiny buttons. Stuffing the silk tails into her skirt, she returned to the living room.

"Yes," she said crisply. "What is it?"

Blake turned around with a slightly guilty look. "I'd say this is a little small, wouldn't you?" He held up one of the dresses she'd purchased for June's baby.

"It's not for me," she said stiffly, refusing to meet his laughing eyes.

"I'd guessed as much," he returned seriously. "Is all this for little Cassi?"

Caasi jerked the dress out of his hands and stuffed it back into its paper sack. "That's none of your business," she declared hotly. "And don't you dare . . ." She paused to inhale a quivering breath. "Don't you *dare* say I'm buying myself a family."

"You *are* their family, Cupcake," Blake said gently.

Caasi jerked her face up and their eyes met. His were warm and oddly indulgent. She wanted to scream at him not to look at her like that. How could he? Only hours before, he'd told her he wanted nothing more to do with her or the Empress. He was the one who wanted out, not her. God knew she didn't want him to go.

Abruptly, Caasi turned away. "Was there something you wanted to tell me?" she asked in a clipped, businesslike tone.

"Yes." Blake walked to the other side of the room and ran his hand through his hair. "Harris won't be able to go with you tomorrow. His son's involved in a high-school championship baseball game. So it looks like you're stuck with me for one last trip."

Terrific, her mind threw out sarcastically.

Some of her thoughts must have shown in her expression. "Don't look so pleased," Blake chided. "We'll be back tomorrow afternoon. I assume after all these years that we can manage to get along for a few hours."

"Sure." The word nearly stuck in her throat, then came out sounding scratchy and weak. "Why not?"

"You tell me," Blake said in a low voice.

Caasi pivoted sharply and walked to her favorite place by the window. "No reason," she said and shrugged her shoulders.

"I'll see you in the morning, then."

Without turning around, she answered, "It looks that way." She stood poised, waiting for the click of the door. When it didn't come, she turned to find Blake watching her.

"Caasi?"

"Was there something else?" she asked politely.

His searching eyes narrowed on her, and Caasi had the impression he wanted to say something more. "No." He shook his head. "I'll see you tomorrow."

"Fine."

Edie was already seated in the dining room when Caasi arrived. Caasi returned her small wave as she entered the room.

"You look positively . . ." Edie paused and sighed longingly. *"Skinny."*

Caasi laughed. "You always did have a smooth tongue."

"The only reason I'm so candid is that for every ounce you've lost, I've gained three." Elbows on the table, Edie leaned forward. "I'm telling you, Caasi, I'm going crazy."

"What's wrong?" Edie had always been the dramatic one, so Caasi wasn't overly concerned.

"Well, for one thing, I can't stop eating peanut butter. I woke up at two this morning and ate it straight out of the jar. Fredd couldn't believe it."

"At least peanut butter is a high source of protein."

Edie groaned and closed her eyes. "That's what Fredd keeps telling me."

"Why the worry?"

"My dear Caasi, have you any idea how fattening peanut butter is?"

"I haven't checked out any calorie counters lately," Caasi responded and fought to hide the smile that teased the corners of her mouth.

"Well, it's fattening, believe me. The shocking thing is I've hated the stuff since I was a kid."

"There are worse things." Caasi attempted to soothe a few of Edie's doubts.

"Okay," Edie agreed and took a sip from her cocktail. "Listen to *this*. I was watching the Blazers play basketball the other night. The center missed two free throws at the foul line and all of a sudden tears welled in my eyes and I started crying. Not just a few silent tears, but gigantic sobs. Fredd didn't know what to think. He was finishing up a report in his den and came rushing in. I'm sure he thought the telecast had been interrupted and someone had just announced that my mother had died or something."

The small laugh could no longer be contained. "Listen, Edie, I'm no expert on the subject, but isn't this all part of being pregnant?"

"Dear Lord, I hope so," Edie said fervently.

"Have you talked to June? She'd probably be more help than me."

"June," Edie repeated and shook her head dramatically. "You know June; she's the salt of the earth. The entire time she was pregnant she acted as if she was in heaven. June's the kind of woman who would deliver her baby and go back to work in the fields an hour later. *I'm* going to need six months' rest on the Riviera to recover."

The maitre d' handed them the menu and gave Caasi a polite nod of recognition.

Edie opened the menu, took one look, moaned, and folded it closed.

"What's the matter?" Caasi asked.

"I was afraid this would happen. Everything looks divine. I want the first four entrees and chocolate mousse for dessert."

"Edie!" Caasi couldn't prevent her small gasp of shock. Of the three, Edie had always been the most weight-conscious.

"I can't help it," Edie hissed.

"If you eat that much, *I'll* get sick."

"All right, all right," Edie said, "you choose for me. I don't trust myself."

The waiter took their order and filled their coffee cups.

"Enough about me." Edie took a sip from the steaming cup. "I want to hear what's been going on in your life. I don't suppose you've picked up any tall, dark, handsome men lately, have you?"

Caasi shrugged and looked away uncomfortably. "Not recently. You know I went into the delivery room with June and Burt, don't you?"

"Don't tell me a thing about it. I don't want to hear." Edie shook her head and squinted her eyes closed.

"It was one of the most beautiful experiences of my life," Caasi reminisced softly.

"Sure—it wasn't *you* going through all that pain."

Caasi didn't bother to try to explain. Edie wouldn't understand. At least, not until her own baby was delivered.

"Have you had any thoughts about what I was saying the last time we were together?" At Caasi's blank look, Edie continued, "You know, about having an affair and maybe getting pregnant yourself?"

Caasi nearly choked on her coffee. "Edie, I wish you wouldn't talk like that."

"Maybe not, but it's what you need. I bet you've lost five pounds since the last time I saw you. Believe me when I tell you a man can do wonders."

"Maybe," Caasi conceded, feeling the color seep up her neck.

"I take it that it didn't work out with the hunk you met here the last time?"

Caasi's hands surrounded her glass of water. She stared at the melting ice and felt the cold move up her arm and stop directly at her heart. "No. It didn't work out."

"It was only your first try, so don't let it discourage you. Would you like me to pick out someone else?"

"No," Caasi returned forcefully. "I'm perfectly capable of finding a man myself. If I want one."

"*If?*"

Their dinner arrived, and thankfully Caasi was able to steer the conversation from Edie's questions to the light banter they normally enjoyed.

After their dinner they decided to have an after-dinner drink in the lounge. The same piano player was at the keyboard and a fresh crowd was gathered around the bar.

The cocktail waitress brought their drinks as Caasi and Edie sat listening to the mellow sounds of a love song.

"Hey," Edie whispered excitedly. "Don't turn around now, but guess who just came in!"

"Who? The Easter Bunny?"

"No," Edie remarked seriously. Her eyes didn't waver. "Mr. Incredible."

"Who?" Caasi whispered.

"The same guy who was here the other night. You remember—you've got to," Edie admonished, her voice dipping incredulously.

Caasi moved her chair so that she could look at the newcomer. She didn't need a second guess to know it was Blake.

Edie's eyes widened appreciatively. "He really is something, isn't he?"

"If you go for that type," Caasi replied with a flippancy she wasn't feeling.

"He's everyone's type," Edie said without taking her eyes off Blake. "Did you notice how every woman here perked up the minute he walked in?"

Caasi certainly had. Her stomach felt as if a hole was being seared through it. The burning sensation didn't lessen when a tall, attractive blond slid onto the empty stool beside Blake. Caasi's eyes narrowed as the woman took out a cigarette and gestured to Blake for a light.

"Watch," Edie advised. "This blonde knows what she's doing. You might be able to pick up a few pointers."

Caasi smiled weakly, her fingers linked into a hard fist in her lap. For one crazy moment she felt like screaming in outrage. Blake was hers! But he wasn't, not really—he had made that clear that morning. Rather than watch the exchange between the two, she lowered her gaze to her Singapore sling.

"Well, I'll be," Edie murmured unbelievingly.

"What?" Caasi demanded.

"Weren't you watching?"

"No," Caasi whispered, her voice shaking.

"As slick as a whistle, Mr. Incredible gave the blond the brush-off. I wouldn't have believed it. This fellow is one tough character. Little wonder you didn't have any luck."

"Little wonder," Caasi repeated.

Edie continued to study Blake. "You know, just watching Mr. Incredible I'm getting the distinct impression he's hurting."

"Hurting?" Caasi asked and swallowed tightly.

"Yes. Look at the way he's leaning against the counter. See the way his elbows are positioned? He doesn't want to be disturbed and his body is saying as much, discouraging anyone from joining him."

"Why doesn't he just sit at a table?" Caasi whispered, revealing her curiosity.

"Because that would be an open invitation for company. No, this man wants to be left alone."

"Just because he wants his own company doesn't mean he's eating his heart out."

Thoughtfully, Edie shook her head. "That's true. But he's troubled. Look at the way he's hunched over his drink. He looks as if he's lost his best friend."

Caasi felt Edie's slow appraisal turn to her. "So do you, for that matter."

"So do I—what?" Caasi feigned ignorance on a falsely cheerful note.

"Never mind," Edie murmured thoughtfully.

"I was looking through some travel brochures the other day . . ." Caasi quickly changed the subject before Edie managed to stumble onto something she could only escape by blatantly lying. "Do you realize I haven't had a vacation, a *real* vacation," she amended, "in over five years? I was thinking of a cruise."

"I'll believe it when I see it." Edie tilted her chin mockingly. "You wouldn't know what to do with yourself with empty time on your hands."

"Sure I would," Caasi argued. "I'd take a few classes. I've always wanted to learn how to do calligraphy. And get back to reading. I bet there are a hundred books I haven't had time to read in the last five years. They're stacked to the ceiling in my bedroom just waiting for me. I'd bake, and learn how to sew, and volunteer some time at the local—" She stopped abruptly at the peculiar look Edie was giving her.

"I can't believe this is Caasi Crane speaking!" Edie looked shocked.

Caasi laughed, hoping to make light of her own enthusiasm and squelch Edie's growing curiosity. "It's been on my mind a lot, that's all."

"What's been on your mind?" Edie asked. "Those weren't things you'd do on vacation. They're things an everyday housewife does."

"A housewife?" She gave Edie a surprised look. "And what's wrong with a housewife?"

"Nothing." Edie was quick to amend her attitude. "Heavens, June's one, and I'll be one shortly. Think about it, Caasi. You, a housewife? A baby on each hip, diapers that need to be folded stacked on the kitchen table. Dinner boiling on top of the stove. Can you picture yourself in that scene?"

Caasi pressed her mouth tightly closed. She longed to cry out that she'd never wanted anything more. If she could run ten hotels effectively, she could manage a single home. The only condition her mind demanded was that Blake share that loving picture with her. Her eyes drifted across the room to the dejected figure sitting at the bar. It took everything within her not to go to him. But she couldn't see that it would do any good. She'd bared her heart and he'd rejected her. Just remembering the shock she'd felt at hearing his decision caused her to bite into her bottom lip.

"Caasi?" Edie's soft voice broke into her musings.

Gently Caasi shook her head. "Sorry." She turned her attention back to Edie. "What were you saying?"

Edie's attention was focused in the direction of the bar. "Look who's coming our way," she whispered in shocked disbelief.

Blake strolled to their table and nodded politely at Edie. "We didn't set a time for tomorrow morning. Is eight too early?"

"Fine." Caasi managed to answer with some difficulty.

"I'll see you then."

Edie looked stunned as Blake turned and walked away. "All right, Caasi Crane," she whispered in a shocked voice, "you've got some explaining to do."

Chapter Eight

The whirling blades of the helicopter stirred the early morning air. With her purse clutched under her arm and her head bowed, Caasi rushed across the landing pad. Blake supported her elbow as she climbed aboard.

The volume of swirling sound made conversation impossible, which was just as well. There was little Caasi had to say to Blake. Not anymore. A week before, even less, she would have been excited about this trip with him. It would have been a chance to talk, another opportunity to learn more about this man who had been invaluable to her for the past five years. Now it would be torture to sit beside him and know that the next day he would be walking out of her life.

"Caasi."

Blake's hand against her forearm recalled her from her musings.

"It's not too late. We can make the drive in less than—"

"No," she interrupted him and, closing her eyes, leaned her head back against the seat cushion. When they'd met at eight that morning, the first thing Blake had done was propose that they drive instead of taking the helicopter. Caasi couldn't understand why he would make such a suggestion. He wasn't any more eager to spend time alone with her than she was to endure the stilted silence that would have existed in the comparative quiet of a car.

When they didn't take off immediately, Caasi opened her eyes and noted that Blake was talking to the pilot. A frown creased his brow before he nodded abruptly and climbed back aboard.

"Is everything all right?" she asked.

"Nothing to worry about," Blake assured her.

A wobbly sensation attacked her stomach as the helicopter rose. To hide her anxiety, Caasi clenched her hands, closed her eyes, and turned her head as if she were gazing out the window.

Blake placed his hand over hers; Caasi sat up and shook her hand free. She didn't want his comfort or assurance or anything else. The day was torture. If he was going to get out of her life, then he should go. Why prolong the agony?

They didn't say a word as Portland disappeared. A small smile flickered across Caasi's face at the memory of Edie's reaction when Blake had stopped at their table the night before. Her friend had been stunned speechless. Caasi couldn't remember a time in all the years they'd known each other that Edie didn't have an immediate comeback.

"You sly fox," Edie had gasped a full minute after Blake had sauntered away from the table.

"Don't get excited," Caasi returned with a nervous smile. "Blake's been around for eight years."

Edie shook her head in disbelief. "You have worked with that hunk all these years?"

"His last day is Wednesday." Something in Caasi's voice must have revealed the pain she felt at the thought.

Edie's look was thoughtful. "I noticed something was different almost from the moment you came into the dining room tonight. At first I was sure I was imagining things. Somehow, you're . . . softer. It's in your eyes, even in the way you walk, if that's possible. You have, my dear, dear Caasi, the look of a woman in love."

Caasi tried to laugh off Edie's announcement. "Who, me?"

"Yes, you!" Edie declared adamantly. "Now tell me, why is Blake leaving?"

Sadly Caasi shook her head. "I don't know. I've tried everything I know to convince him to stay."

"Everything?"

Hot color suffused Caasi's face and she lowered her gaze, unable to meet Edie's probing eyes. "It wouldn't do any good. Blake's mind is set."

"Is there any chance of you two getting together?"

Caasi shook her head, unable to answer with words. A terrible sadness settled over her heart. The pain was as potent as it had been at her father's death. In some ways, the hurt was the same. Blake would be lost to her. Just as she would never have her father again, she would never have Blake.

"What about your baby hunger?" Edie asked.

"My what?" Caasi jerked her head up.

"The last time we were together we talked about you and a baby, don't you remember?"

"Yes, but a baby usually requires a father."

Edie gave a sophisticated shrug. "Not always. You're a successful career woman. You're strong, independent, and financially capable. Any child would be lucky to have you as a mother."

"I can't believe what I'm hearing." Caasi gripped her hands in her lap so that Edie wouldn't see how her fingers were trembling. "You're not really suggesting I get pregnant with Blake's child?"

"Of course I am. He's leaving, isn't he? You want a baby, not a husband. As far as I can see, the setup is perfect."

Even now, with Blake sitting beside her, Caasi couldn't help shaking her head in disbelief at her friend's suggestion. Sometimes it was astonishing that two women so completely different could be such good friends.

An hour later, with a cup of coffee in front of her, Caasi reviewed the architects' plans. The piece of beach was prime property, and Caasi realized how fortunate she was to have obtained it. No, she had Blake to thank for that. He was the one who had handled the negotiations.

Seaside was a tourist town. The economy depended

on the business of travelers. With only a few weeks left until summer and a flux of vacationers, the community was preparing for the seasonal traffic.

The morning passed quickly. Leaving the architects' office, Caasi donned a hard hat and visited the building site. Everything was ahead of schedule; where she had pitched a shovelful of dirt only a few weeks before now stood the empty shell of the latest Empress Hotel.

Caasi walked around, examining each area. Once she would have experienced an intense satisfaction at the venture; now she was surprised to feel nothing. The lack of emotion shocked her. What did she care if there were ten or a hundred Empress Hotels? Would breaking ground for another hotel bring her happiness? Perhaps at one time it would have. But no longer. Blake was responsible for that. He was responsible for a lot of things.

The smile felt frozen on her lips as she entered the restaurant where the chamber of commerce was holding its luncheon.

After they ate, Caasi stood before the group and spoke a few introductory words before turning the presentation over to Blake. As he was talking, Caasi observed the way the men in the room responded to him. In some ways their reactions were like those of the women in the cocktail lounge the night before. Blake was a man's man. The magnetism about him defied barriers.

Caasi's fingers were tender from all the handshaking she'd done by the time they returned to the copter. The pilot, a middle-aged man with a receding hair line, removed his hat as they approached. He shook his head, seeking Blake's eyes.

"Is something wrong?" Caasi asked Blake.

"I don't know, but I'll find out."

Blake and the pilot talked for several minutes and when Blake returned, his jaw was tight, his look disturbed.

"Well?"

"There's something wrong with the chopper. Dick noticed that one of the gauges was malfunctioning when he revved it up this morning. That was why I suggested we drive."

Caasi closed her mouth tightly to bite back bitter words. Blake hadn't been eager for her company that morning. Had she been fooling herself with the belief that he would have enjoyed an intimate drive from Portland?

"How long will it take to check it out?"

"An hour, two at the most."

Unwilling to spend an extra minute in Blake's company, Caasi announced, "I'll wait for you on the beach, then."

Blake didn't acknowledge her as she turned and walked the block or so to the ocean.

Wind whipped her hair about her face as she stood looking out over the pounding surf.

A flight of concrete stairs led to the beach. Caasi walked down to the sand, removed her heels, and strolled toward the water until her nylons felt the moisture.

Once, when she was a little girl, her father had taken her to the ocean. A business trip, Caasi was sure. Very little in Isaac Crane's life had been done for pleasure. Caasi could recall vividly how the thundering surf had frightened her and how she'd clung to her father's leg.

Funny, Caasi mused, she hadn't thought about that in years. She couldn't have been more than two, maybe three, at the time. The incident was her earliest memory.

Swinging her high heels in her hands, Caasi walked for what seemed like miles, enjoying the solitude, the fresh, salt-scented air, and the peace that came over her. Blake would go and she'd hurt for a time, suffer through the regrets for the love they could have shared. But the time would come when that, too, would pass. And she'd be better for having loved him.

When she turned around to return to the street, she noticed Blake standing at the top of the concrete steps watching her. He was a solitary figure silhouetted against the bright sun, hands in his pockets and at ease with the world. That disturbed her somehow. He was leaving her without a second thought, without regrets, without looking back.

As she neared the steps, Blake came down to meet her. "I just talked to Dick."

"And?" she prompted.

"The problem is more extensive than he thought. It looks as if we'll have to spend the night."

"Spend the night?" she cried in frustration. "I won't do that."

"There isn't much choice," Blake returned with limited patience.

"Rent a car. And if you can't do that, then buy one! I'm not spending the night here."

THE TROUBLE WITH CAASI

"Caasi." Blake drew in a slow, angry breath.

"You're still my employee," she said bitterly and glanced at her watch. "For another twenty-three and a half hours I expect you to do what I say. After that, I don't give a damn."

Caasi regretted the words the minute they slipped out. She watched Blake's struggle to hide his anger. His fists knotted at his sides until his knuckles were white.

"I didn't mean that," she said in a low voice and released her breath slowly. "Make what arrangements you can. I'll phone Louise and answer any necessary calls from here."

Fifteen minutes later Caasi walked across her hotel room, carrying the phone with her as she spoke. A knock on her door interrupted the conversation.

"Could you hold a minute, Louise?" she asked before unlocking the door and letting Blake into the rented quarters.

"It's Blake," she said into the receiver. "I'll give you a call in the morning before we leave." She hung up and turned to him. "Yes?"

"I thought you might need a few things." He handed her a small sack that contained a toothbrush and toothpaste.

"Thanks." She smiled her appreciation. "But what I could really use is a good martini."

"Dry, of course."

"Very dry," Caasi agreed.

The cocktail lounge was deserted; it was too early for the predinner crowd and too late for the business-luncheon group.

It amazed Caasi that they could sit companionably

at a minuscule table and not say a word. It was almost as if they were an old married couple who no longer needed words to communicate. Caasi focused her attention on the ocean scene outside the window. The view was lovely, but she had seen so much breathtaking scenery in her life. That day it failed to stir the familiar chord of appreciation.

Without asking, Blake ordered another round of martinis for them. Slowly, Caasi sipped her drink. The bitter liquid seared its way down her throat. The lounge was quickly filling now; after two martinis Caasi could feel the coiled tension ease out of her.

"Are you ready for dinner?" Blake asked.

"Sure," she agreed readily, "why not?"

His hand cupped her elbow as he escorted her into the dining room. The food was good, though not excellent.

"I should have Chef share some of his recipes," Caasi remarked as she set her fork aside.

"You and that damn chef. I don't know when I was more upset with you than when you imported him."

Caasi's smile didn't quite reach her eyes. "Oh, I can tell you. Several times you've looked as if you wanted to wring my neck, all within the last couple of weeks too."

Blake's expression was weary and he conceded her observation with a short shake of his head.

The soulful sounds of a singer drifted into the dining room from the lounge.

"Shall we?" Blake asked softly.

Caasi couldn't find an excuse to refuse. All there was to do in her room was watch television. "All right," she agreed, somewhat reluctantly. When they reentered the lounge, she saw that a few couples occupied the tiny dance floor, which was little bigger than a tabletop.

They sat for a long time, so close their thighs were touching, listening to the music and not speaking. For the first time Caasi admitted to herself how glad she was that the helicopter needed work. The repairs afforded her this last chance to be with Blake. She didn't speak for a long time, fearing words would destroy the moment.

"Caasi."

Their eyes met and she drew a shaky breath at the intensity of his look.

"Dance with me, Blake," she whispered urgently. "Hold me one last time."

He answered her by standing and giving her his hand. They didn't take their eyes from one another as Caasi slid her arms around his neck, her body's movement joining his in a rhythm that was uniquely theirs.

His fingers were pressed against the small of her back as he molded her to him. His mouth was mere inches from hers as his warm breath fanned her cheek.

The music stopped—but they didn't. If Blake released her now, she'd die, Caasi mused.

She released an uneven breath when the singer began again. A love song. Caasi bit into the corner of her bottom lip and sighed. Tomorrow Blake would go—but for tonight he was hers.

Caasi lost track of how long Blake held her, how many songs they danced to, barely moving, oblivious to the world surrounding them.

When the music stopped, Caasi led the way off the

dance floor, but instead of stopping at their table she continued out of the lounge and down the wide hall to their rooms, which were opposite one another.

Her hands shook as she inserted the key and opened the door to her room. It was dark and silent.

Blake's dark eyes bore into hers as she stepped inside the room and extended her hand to him. A look of indecision passed across his face. Caasi's eyes pleaded with him, and gradually the expression on his face softened as his look became potent enough for her to drown in.

He took one step inside and Caasi released a deep sigh of relief. He couldn't turn away from her. Not now. Not tonight.

She slid her arms around his neck and stood on the tips of her toes as she melted against him.

He groaned her name, reaching out to close the door as she fit her body to his.

She wouldn't let him talk, her open mouth seeking his. He hadn't kissed her in so long, so very long.

"Caasi." He groaned, repeatedly rubbing his mouth over hers. "You don't know what you're doing." His voice was husky and hungry.

"I do," she insisted in a low murmur. "Oh, Blake, I do."

Again and again his mouth cherished hers, eager, hungry, seeking, demanding, giving, taking. The soft, gentle sounds of their lovemaking filled the silence. They whispered phrases of awe as passion took control of their bodies.

Caasi paused long enough to tug the shirt free at

Blake's waist. Eagerly her fingers fumbled with the buttons until she could slip her palms over his chest. The sensations were so exquisite she wanted to cry.

"Caasi, no," Blake whispered gruffly. "Not now, not like this." The shirt fell to the floor.

"Yes, like this," she pleaded. "Only tonight, it's all I want." She felt the tears well in her eyes. Her body trembled wildly against his, and Blake released an anguished groan as he swung her off her feet and carried her across the room.

Caasi wanted him so desperately, she could no longer think. Pressing her face to his neck, she gave him tiny, biting kisses and felt his shudder as he laid her on the bed.

Her arms around his neck, Caasi refused to release him, half lifting herself as she kissed him long and hard, her mouth slanting under his.

His eyes looked tortured in the golden glow of the moon as he pulled her arms from his neck. "Caasi," he whispered in a voice she hardly recognized. "Are you drunk? Is this the liquor?"

"Yes, I'm drunk," she whispered, "but not from the martinis. You do this to me, Blake. Only you."

"This isn't the way I wanted it, but God knows I haven't got the strength to let you go," he murmured, his lips above hers. His hands ran down her smooth body, exploring, touching, until Caasi was sure she would die if he didn't take her. She arched against him and sighed with a longing so intense that it sounded like a mournful cry.

Impatient male hands worked at her clothing, freeing her from the constricting material. The feel of his hands against her bare skin was an exquisite torture.

"Tonight," she whispered in a quivering breath. "For tonight, I'm yours."

"Yes," he agreed, his mouth seeking hers again.

"I'm freeing you from any . . . consequences." She stammered slightly.

He froze. For a moment he didn't even breathe. "You're what?" He sat up, holding her away from him, a rough hand against each bare shoulder.

"I'm freeing you from any responsibility," she murmured, confused. What had she said that upset him so much? Wasn't that something a man wanted to hear?

Sitting on the edge of the bed, Blake leaned forward and buried his face in his hands as if he needed time to compose himself.

"Blake," she pleaded in a soft whisper, "what did I say?"

He didn't answer as he reached for his shirt and rammed his arms into the sleeves. Not bothering to fasten the buttons, he started across the room.

"Blake," she begged, "don't do this to me. Please don't do this to me."

He turned to her in the moonlight. She had never seen a man look more angry. His face was white with rage, his mouth twisted, his eyes as hard as flint.

Caasi sagged against the bed, closing her eyes against the searing pain that went through her heart, a pain so deep that it was beyond tears.

For hours Caasi lay exactly as she was, staring

dry-eyed at the ceiling. She had offered Blake everything she had to give and he had rejected it all.

Even her makeup couldn't camouflage the dark circles under her eyes the next morning. The mirror revealed pale, colorless cheeks, as if she were recovering from a long illness. Caasi doubted that she would ever recover. Not really. She'd go on with her life, would probably even laugh again, but something deep inside her had died last night. In some respects she would never be the same again.

It gave her little satisfaction to note that Blake looked as if he hadn't slept either.

Dick was at the helicopter when they arrived, assuring them that everything was fixed and ready to go.

Blake didn't offer her his hand when she climbed inside, which was just as well, since she would have refused it. They sat as far apart from each other as possible.

The atmosphere was so thick that even Dick was affected, glancing anxiously from one to the other, then concentrating on the flight.

As Caasi ran the bath water in her quarters back at the Empress, she realized there was nothing about the short flight home that she could remember. The pain of being so close to Blake was almost more than she could bear. Her mind had blotted it from her memory.

Blake had stepped out of the helicopter and announced stiffly that he was going home to change and would be back later to clear out his desk and pack up what remained of his personal items. It was Wednesday. His last day with Crane Enterprises.

Caasi hadn't bothered to answer him but had turned and gone directly to her suite.

Some of the staff had planned a small farewell party for Blake, but she hadn't contributed anything. Not when seeing him go was so painful. There would be an obligatory statement of good wishes she would make. Somehow she'd manage that. Somehow.

A hot bath relieved some of the tiredness in her bones, but it had little effect on her heart.

Dressed in a prim business suit, Caasi walked briskly into the office and offered Louise a short nod before entering her own.

Her desk was stacked with mail, telephone messages, and a variety of items that needed her immediate attention.

"Louise," she called to her secretary, "send in Brian Harris."

"Right away."

If the man was there to take Blake's place, she had best start working with him now.

By noon Caasi's head was pounding. She wasn't one to suffer from headaches, but the pain was quickly becoming unbearable.

"Are you all right?" Louise asked as she came into Caasi's office for dictation.

"I'm fine," Caasi said with a weak smile. She stood at the window, her fingertips massaging her temples as she shot off one letter after another, scarcely pausing between items of correspondence.

Louise sat on the edge of her chair, her glasses delicately balanced on the bridge of her nose as her pencil flew across the steno pad.

"That'll be all." Caasi paused. "No; get me Dirk Evans of International on the phone."

Louise returned to her office and buzzed Caasi a minute later. "Mr. Evans is on line two."

"Thanks, Louise," Caasi said with a sigh. "Would it be possible for you to find me some aspirin?"

"Of course."

"Thanks." Five years since she took over for her father, and this was the first time she'd ever needed anything to help her through the day.

The aspirin had little effect on the pounding sensation that persisted at her temples well into the afternoon.

Louise came into her office around four to tell her that the farewell party for Blake was in progress.

"I'll be there in a minute," Caasi said without looking up, her fingers tightening around her pen.

Hands braced against the side of her desk, Caasi inhaled deeply, closing her eyes and forcing herself to absorb the silence for a couple of moments before rising and going to join the party.

Someone had opened a bottle of champagne. Caasi stood on the outskirts of the small crowd and watched as everyone toasted Blake and wished him success. One of the women had made a farewell cake and was serving thin slices. Caasi recognized her as Blake's personal secretary but couldn't recall her being so attractive.

Caasi felt far removed from the joking banter that existed between Blake and his staff. There wasn't one who didn't regret his leaving. Yet he had chosen to do exactly that.

Someone slapped him across the back and he laughed but stopped short as his eyes met hers.

Quickly Caasi looked away. A hush fell over the room as she walked to the center, Blake at her side.

"I think we can all agree that you'll be missed," she said in a voice that was surprisingly steady. "If my father were here I'm sure he would say how much he appreciated the excellent job you have done for Crane Enterprises for the past eight years. I'm sure he'd extend to you his personal best wishes."

"But not yours?" Blake whispered for her ears alone.

Stiffening, Caasi continued somewhat defiantly, "My own are extended to you in whatever you pursue. If there's ever a time you feel you'd like to return, you know that there will always be a place for you here. Good-bye, Blake."

"What? No gold watch?" he mumbled under his breath as he stepped forward and shook her hand. "Thank you, Miss Crane." Those dark, unreadable eyes stared into hers, and Caasi could barely breathe.

Grateful for the opportunity to escape, she nodded and stepped aside as Blake's secretary approached with a small wrapped package. Hoping to give the impression she was needed elsewhere, Caasi glanced at her watch. "If you'll excuse me, please."

"Of course." Blake answered for the group.

Without another word, she turned and walked away, not stopping until she reached her desk.

Caasi forced herself to eat some dinner. For two days she hadn't been able to force down more than a few bites of any meal.

The headache was now forty-eight hours old. Nothing seemed to relieve the throbbing pain. She hadn't slept well either. After several hours of tossing fitfully she would fall into an uneasy slumber, only to wake an hour or two later more tired than when she'd gone to bed.

The phone rang Saturday when she returned from a spot check at the Sacramento Empress.

"Hello," she said, with little enthusiasm.

"Is this Caasi?"

Faintly Caasi recognized the voice over the phone. Her home phone had a private listing and she seldom gave out the number.

"Yes, it is."

"Caasi." The young voice sounded relieved. "This is Gina. Gina Sherrill."

"Hello, Gina. What can I do for you?" Caasi's hand tightened around the receiver. The girl had phoned three times in the last few days, and Caasi hadn't returned the calls. She had completely severed herself from Blake and wanted every painful reminder of him removed from her life.

"I'm sorry to bother you like this, but I haven't been able to get hold of you at your office."

"I've been busy lately." She hoped the tone of her

voice would effectively convey the message. She didn't want to be purposely rude to the girl.

"I knew that, and I hope you'll forgive me for being so forward, but I did want to tell you that everyone would like it if you could come to dinner on Sunday."

Everyone but Blake, Caasi added silently. "I'm sure I'd like that very much, but I'm sorry, it's impossible this week. Perhaps another time."

Caasi heard a sigh of disappointment come over the line. "I understand."

Maybe she did, Caasi mused.

"I'd like to talk to you someday when you've got the time."

"I'd enjoy that, Gina, but I really am busy. Thank you for calling. Give my love to your family."

"I will. Good-bye, Caasi."

Caasi heard the drone of the disconnected line sound in her ear. Replacing the receiver, she walked to the window and studied the view of miniature people and miniature cars far below.

Someone knocked on her door, and she wanted to cry out in irritation. Why couldn't people just leave her alone? Everything would be fine if she could have some peace and quiet in her life.

"Just a minute," she answered shortly as she strode across the floor. She opened the door to discover . . . Blake. Her heart leapt into her throat, and she was too stunned to move.

"I hope you haven't eaten yet. By the way, where were you all afternoon?" he asked as he walked past her into the living room.

Chapter Nine

"Where was I?" Caasi repeated, nonplussed. What was Blake doing here? Hadn't he left her, decided to sever his relationship with her and Crane Enterprises?

"Yes—I've been trying to get you all day."

Her hand on the door knob, Caasi watched his relaxed movements as he sauntered to the sofa, sat back, and positioned his ankle on his knee.

"I do have a business to run." She hated the telltale way her voice shook, revealing her shock.

"Yes, but it wasn't business that kept you out. I know, because I checked."

"You checked?" Caasi demanded. "Then I suggest you question your sources, because it most certainly *was* business."

"Instead of standing all the way over there and

arguing, why don't you come and sit with me?" He held out his hand invitingly. "I certainly hope you're hungry, because I'm starved."

Caasi closed the door but didn't sit with him as he requested. Instead she walked to the window, her arms cradling her waist.

"What you're wearing is fine," he assured her. "Don't bother to change."

Her gaze shot to him. The friendly, almost gentle light in his eyes was enough to steal her breath. His ready smile was warm and encouraging.

"I thought you wanted out of Crane Enterprises."

"I did."

"Then why are you here? Why come back? Don't you know how hard it was for me to let you walk away? Are you really that insensitive, Blake? I don't want you flitting in and out of my life when the mood strikes you. I haven't seen you in . . ."

"Three days," he supplied. "I know. I wanted you to have time to think things through, but I can see you haven't figured anything out yet."

Caasi's hands became knotted fists and fell to her sides. "I hate it when people play these kinds of games with me. If you have something to say, then for God's sake, say it."

Blake released a frustrated sigh. "Are you really so dense you can't see?"

"I don't need to stand in my own home and be insulted by you, Blake Sherrill." She stalked across the room and opened the door. "Perhaps it would be best if you left."

"Caasi." A hint of anger reverberated in his husky voice. "I didn't come here to argue."

"Well, you seem to be doing a bang-up job of it."

He stood and rammed his hands into his pockets. He strode to the window, his back to her as he gazed at the panorama.

Caasi could see and feel the frustration in the rigid set of his shoulders. She didn't want to fight. The desire to walk to him and slip her arms around his waist and press her face to his back was almost overwhelming. The headache that had persisted since Blake left was her body's method of telling her how miserable she had been without him. A hundred times since Wednesday she'd had to stop herself from consulting him, remembering that Blake was no longer available to ask. Softly she exhaled and closed the door.

At the sound of the click, Blake turned around. "Can we start again, Cupcake? Pretend I'm an old friend who's come to town for the weekend."

Caasi lowered her gaze. "Don't call me Cupcake," she murmured stiffly. "I'm not a little girl. That's the last way I want you to think of me."

The sound of his robust laugh filled the room. "There's no worry of that."

Indecision gripped Caasi. All her life she'd been in control of every situation. She had always known what to expect and how to react. But not with Blake and this new ground he seemed to want to travel with her. Of one thing Caasi was sure: she couldn't tolerate much more of the pain he inflicted when he walked away.

"Dinner, Caasi?" His arched brow contained a challenging lift.

Her compliant nod was as weak as her resolve. She

would accept what little Blake was willing to offer and be grateful.

His smile crinkled the lines at his eyes. "Come on; I've got fat steaks ready for the barbecue."

Caasi took a light jacket out of the closet. "Where are we going?"

"To my place."

"Your place?"

"Then after dinner I thought we'd try our luck at the horse races."

"Horse races?" she repeated.

Blake looked around, stared at the ceiling, and shook his head. "This room seems to have developed an echo all of a sudden."

Caasi smiled. It was the first time she could remember smiling since Monday, when Blake had announced he would be leaving her and Crane Enterprises.

They rode in his T-Bird convertible with the top down. The wind ruffled her sleekly styled curls, and Caasi closed her eyes to savor the delicious sensations that flowed through her. She was with Blake, and it felt so right.

The barbecue could be seen in the back yard, a bag of briquets leaning against its base, when Blake pulled into the driveway. He came around and opened her car door for her. Leaning over the rolled-down window, he lightly brushed his mouth across hers. He straightened and his eyes looked deeply into hers. With a groan his arms surrounded her, half lifting her from the car as she arched against the muscular wall of his chest. Caasi slipped her arms around his neck and surrendered fully to the mastery of his kiss. Gradually his grip relaxed and he tenderly brushed the tangled hair from her temple. "I've missed you."

Still caught in the rush of emotion he could evoke, Caasi didn't speak. A happy smile lifted the corners of her mouth in a trembling smile. "I've missed you too."

"I'll cook the steaks if you fix the salad. Agreed?"

Eagerly, Caasi nodded. He helped her out of the car, his arm cupping her shoulder as he led her up the back stairs and into the kitchen.

"I'll get the barbecue going and leave you to your task," he instructed.

Almost immediately he was out the back door. Taking off her jacket, Caasi draped it over a chair and looked around. She really loved this house. A gentle feeling warmed her. Any woman would be proud to be a part of this.

The ingredients for the salad were in the refrigerator, and she laid them on the counter. Next she searched through the cupboards for a large bowl. A salad shouldn't be difficult, she mused happily. Her culinary skills were limited, but a salad would be easy enough.

She was at the cutting board chopping lettuce when Blake came back for the steaks and a variety of spices.

He paused, watching her as she slid the knife across the fresh lettuce.

"Is something the matter?" She tensed and looped a strand of hair behind her ear. What could she possibly be doing wrong in making a salad? It was the simplest job he could have given her.

"No. It's just that it's better to tear apart the lettuce leaves instead of cutting them."

"Okay." Feeling incredibly naïve in the kitchen, Caasi set the knife aside.

"Did you wash it?" Blake asked her next.

Caasi swallowed at the painful lump that filled her throat. With tight-lipped grimness she answered him by a negative shake of her head. Dumping the cut lettuce into the bowl, she carried it to the sink and filled the bowl with water. Pure pique caused her to pour dishwashing liquid over the green leaves. "Like this?" She batted her long lashes at him innocently.

Not waiting for his reaction, she moved into the living room and stared sightlessly out the front window. A hand over her mouth, she took in several deep breaths. What was she doing here with Blake? This wonderful homey scene wasn't meant for someone like her. She was about as undomesticated as they came.

The sound of footsteps told her Blake had moved behind her. His hand on her shoulder sent a silky warmth sliding down her arm.

"I apologize," she whispered. "That was a stupid thing to do."

"No; I should be the one to apologize." The pressure of his hands turned her around. Gently he pulled her into his arms, his chin resting against the top of her head.

"It's just that I'm so incredibly dumb." Her voice was thick with self-derision.

"You, stupid?" Soft laughter tumbled from his throat, stirring the hair at the crown of her head. "Maybe you won't be competing in the same class as Chef, but not because you lack intelligence. You've just never learned, that's all."

"But will I ever?"

"That's up to you, Cupcake."

Caasi winced. "You're using that name again when I've asked you repeatedly not to."

He didn't comment for several tense moments. "I don't think I'll ever forget the first time I saw you. I'd been working with your father for several months. Isaac didn't talk much about his private life. I think I was at the Empress six months before I even knew he had a daughter. We were in his office one day and you came floating in as fresh as spring and so breathtakingly beautiful I nearly fell out of my chair." He stopped and gently eased her away so that he could look at her as he spoke. "I watched this hard-nosed businessman light up like a sparkler on the Fourth of July. His eyes softened as he held out his arms to you and called you Cupcake. I've never thought of you as anything else since."

"I was only twenty."

A finger under her chin lifted her face to his. "The amazing part is that you're even more beautiful now." Ever so gently, he placed his mouth over hers.

No kiss had ever been so incredibly sweet. Caasi swayed toward him when he released her and sighed with all the love in her heart. "I hope you've got another head of lettuce. I'm afraid I've ruined the first one."

"I'll start cooking the steaks now." He kissed her on the tip of her nose and released her. "How do you want your steak cooked? Rare?"

"No, medium."

Blake looked dissatisfied. "You honestly should try it cooked a little less sometime."

"Blake." She placed her hands on her hips and shook her head. "We seem doomed for one confrontation after another. I happen to prefer my meat medium. If you'd rather, I can cook my own."

"I'd like to see that."

"Steak," she asserted, "I can do. There's nothing to it but flopping it over the grill a couple of times."

"It's an art."

"You overrate yourself," Caasi insisted. "How about I cook the steaks and you make the salad?"

Blake chuckled, shaking his head. "I hate to see good meat wasted, but it'll be worth it just to prove my point."

Caasi was in the back yard readjusting the grill so that it was closer to the fire when Blake walked out.

"I thought you were making the salad."

"I did," he said teasingly, his eyes twinkling. "I slapped a hunk of lettuce on a plate, added a slice of tomato, and poured dressing over the top. What's happening to my steak is of much more interest to me."

"On second thought . . ." Caasi moistened her dry lips. "I'd hate to ruin your meal. Why don't we each cook our own?"

"That sounds fair," Blake agreed with a smile.

The thick steaks sizzled when placed across the grill, flames curling around the edges of fat.

"Who the hell lowered this? It's too close to the fire," he said irritably.

Guiltily, Caasi handed him the potholders she was holding. "Sorry," she muttered.

Blake didn't look pleased. He obviously took his barbecuing seriously. He'd flipped his steak over before Caasi had a chance to add salt and pepper to hers.

When he lifted the barely warmed meat from the grill, Caasi dropped her jaw in disbelief. "That couldn't possibly be done."

"This is a rare steak."

"That's not rare," she declared with tight-lipped insistence. "It's raw. A good vet would have it back on its feet in fifteen minutes."

What had been a light, teasing air was suddenly cold and sober.

"You cook your meat the way you like it and I'll have mine my way. As far as I can see, you're not in any position to tell me what's right or wrong in the kitchen."

Caasi felt the color drain out of her face. Quickly she averted her eyes.

"Caasi," Blake said, forcefully expelling his breath. "I didn't mean that."

"Why not?" She gave a weak smile. "It's true. You go and eat. I'll join you in a few minutes."

Caasi ate little of her dinner and noted that Blake didn't either. Her steak was burned crisp around the edges and was far more well-done than she normally enjoyed. The whole time they were eating she waited for Blake to make some sarcastic comment about her cooking. She was grateful that he didn't.

Blake didn't say anything when she left the table and took her plate to the sink. The bowlful of sudsy lettuce leaves was there to remind her of her childish prank. This new relationship Blake apparently wanted to build wasn't going to work; she couldn't be with him more than ten minutes without fighting. She didn't know how to respond to him on unfamiliar ground. Crane Enterprises had been a common denominator, but now that was gone.

Gathering the wilted greens in her hands, she dumped them into the garbage.

"You could use the disposal instead of . . ."

"I think I've had enough of your 'instead ofs' to last me a lifetime." She made a show of glancing at her watch. "On second thought, maybe we should forego the races for another time."

"I couldn't agree with you more," he snapped. He stood abruptly, almost knocking over his chair in the process. Pointedly he took the car keys from his pocket.

They didn't say a word during the entire drive back to the Empress. Caasi sat upright, her arms crossed determinedly in front of her. The entire evening had been a fiasco.

Blake pulled up to the curb in front of the hotel. His hands clenched the steering wheel as he stared straight ahead. "We need to talk, but now isn't the time. Neither one of us is in the mood for a serious discussion."

Caasi released a pain-filled sigh. "What do you want from me, Blake? When you worked for the hotel I knew exactly where we stood, but now all I feel is an uncertainty I can't explain." She watched as Blake's hand tightened on the wheel until his knuckles were white.

"You haven't figured it out yet? After all these years you still don't know, do you?" He was so angry that Caasi knew any kind of response would only fuel his irritation. "Maybe it is too late, maybe you're so impossibly wrapped up in Crane Enterprises that you'll never know." A resolute hardness closed over his features.

She'd barely closed the car door before he drove away. As the car sped down the street, she stood alone on the deserted sidewalk. Blake was always leaving her.

Later that night, as she lay in bed staring at the dark ceiling, Caasi thought about his parting comment. Obviously she had been horribly wrong not to recognize his motives.

Rather than suffer through another day of self-recrimination over her relationship with Blake, Caasi drove to June and Burt's on Sunday afternoon.

"Welcome," June said and gave Caasi a hug after letting her in the screen door. "I'm glad you came. The first pictures of Cassi have arrived. You wouldn't believe how much she's changed already."

"Sure I would." Caasi walked into the house and handed June a small gift she'd picked up for the baby while in Sacramento.

"Caasi," June protested, "you've got to stop buying Cassi all these gifts. Otherwise, she'll grow up and not appreciate anything."

"Let me spoil her," Caasi pleaded and lifted the sleeping baby from the bassinet. "She's probably the closest thing I'll ever have to a daughter. And I love her so much, it's hard not to."

"I know." June sighed and shook her head in defeat. "But try to hold it down. There isn't any more room in her bedroom to hold all your gifts."

"I hope that's not true."

"Almost," June said. "She's due to wake up any

minute and will probably want to eat. I'll get you a cup of coffee now. Burt's working in the back, putting up one of those aluminum storage sheds."

Cradling the sleeping baby in her arms, Caasi sat in the rocking chair. Her eyes misted as she watched the angelic face. It never failed to materialize, the powerful, overwhelming surge of love she experienced every time she held this child. If this was what she felt with June's baby, how much more would she feel for her own? The question had been on her mind ever since her dinner with Edie. What had Edie called it? Baby hunger. But it was more than that, far more than a passing fancy because her two best friends were having children. When June and Edie had married she hadn't had the urge to go out and find herself a husband. These feelings were different.

A home and family would be worth more than all the accumulated riches of Crane Enterprises. Her father had worked himself into an early grave, and for what reason? All those years he had slaved to build a fortune for her. But she didn't want wealth. The greatest desires of her heart were for a simple life. A home and family, maybe a dog or two. Certainly, money alone couldn't provide all that.

The baby stirred and, opening her tiny mouth, arched her back and yawned.

"Diaper-changing time," Caasi announced as she carried little Cassi into the bedroom and laid her across the changing table. The safety pin slid through the gauze diaper, and within a matter of minutes Caasi handed the baby to her mother.

June sat in a rocking chair and unbuttoned her blouse to nurse. "Every time I see you with the baby I'm amazed at how natural you are with her," June said as she smoothed the soft hairs away from her daughter's face. "To be honest, I was afraid you wouldn't do well around children, but I was wrong. You're a natural. I wish you'd marry and have children of your own."

The coffee cup sat on the end table, and Caasi's hand tightened around it. "I've been giving some serious thought to exactly that."

"Caasi, that's wonderful!" June exclaimed. "You don't know how glad I'll be to see you get away from that hotel. It's dominated your life. I swear, it's been like a monster that's eaten away at you more and more until you were hardly yourself. Who's the lucky man?"

Caasi shifted uncomfortably, crossed and uncrossed her legs, then set her cup aside. "I wasn't thinking of getting married."

June's eyes widened incredulously. "You mean..." She stopped and looked flustered. "You're just going to have a baby?"

"Something like that," Caasi explained cheerfully. "A husband is a nice extra but not necessary."

"I don't get it. Why not marry? You're an attractive woman, and you have so much to offer."

"Maybe," Caasi returned flippantly, "but in this case a husband would be an encumbrance I can live without."

"What about the baby? Doesn't he—or she—have a right to a father?"

"That's something I'm thinking about now."

"This whole idea doesn't even sound like you. Where did you come up with . . ." June stopped, a knowing look lighting her eyes. "Edie. This sounds exactly like one of her crazy schemes."

"Maybe." A smile tugged at the corners of Caasi's mouth. "And when you think about it, the idea isn't all that crazy. Single women are raising children all the time."

"Yes, but . . ." Slowly June shook her head, her eyes narrowing with concern. "Have you chosen the father? I mean, have you said anything to him?"

"Not yet."

"Then you *have* chosen someone?"

"Oh, yes. You've never met him, but he . . ." Caasi paused and swallowed. "He used to work for me. Actually, I think my method is a better idea than Edie's. She suggested I pick up someone in a bar. I swear, that woman is looney sometimes."

"I'm going to have a talk with her," June muttered between tight lips.

"Don't. To be honest, I think she was only kidding. She didn't expect me to take it all so seriously, but I have and I am."

"You know, Caasi, I've never advised you about anything. You've never needed my advice. There's confidence in everything about you—the way you talk, the way you stand, the way you look. Think about this, think very seriously before you do something you might regret all your life."

"I will," Caasi assured her with a warm smile. "I've

never done anything haphazardly in my well-ordered existence, and I'm not about to start now."

Monday's mail included an invitation to Gina and Donald's wedding. She felt badly at having snubbed Blake's sister the past Saturday. Gina was a warm and loving young woman. Caasi took her checkbook and wrote out a generous amount. Staring at the amount, she pictured her confrontation with Blake after she'd sent his cousin a wedding gift. She could imagine what he'd accuse her of if he saw this. Defeated, Caasi tore the check in two and wrote another for half the amount of the first.

"What the heck," she muttered with frustration. What gave Blake Sherrill the right to dictate the amount or kind of gift she gave anyone? Angrily she tore out another check and wrote it out for the amount of the original one. After scribbling an apologetic letter declining the invitation, she added her congratulations and hoped the couple could put the money to good use.

The letter and money went out in the afternoon mail.

Tuesday Caasi met with her lawyer. If he thought her request was a little unusual he said nothing, at least not to her. He did admit, however, that he hadn't handled anything like that in the past and would have to get back to her. Caasi told him there wasn't any rush. She hadn't heard from Blake since their Saturday-night clash.

Wednesday morning Caasi was in her office giving dictation to Louise when Blake burst in.

"There'd better be a damn good explanation for this." He slapped a newspaper on top of her desk.

Completely calm, Caasi turned to Louise. "Maybe it would be best if you excused us for a few moments, Louise. It seems Mr. Sherrill has something he'd like to say."

The secretary stood up, left the office, and closed the door behind her. Blake waited until they were alone.

"Well," he demanded and stalked to the far side of the room.

"I knew this would happen." Her hand gestured impatiently. "I knew the minute I put the money in the mail that you'd come storming in here as if I'd done some terrible deed. Quite frankly, Blake Sherrill, I'm growing weary of your attempts to dictate my life."

"Dictate your life!" he repeated and rammed both hands into his pants pockets, then just as quickly pulled them out again and smoothed back his hair. Even when angry, Blake was a fine male figure. His body was rock hard as he continued to pace the carpet. "I couldn't believe it. I still am having trouble." He stared at her as if he'd never seen her before. "Caasi, what would your father say?" He was deadly serious as his narrowed gaze captured hers.

"My father?" She shook her head in bewilderment. "My father has been dead for five years. I don't think he'd care one way or another if I sent your sister a generous wedding present."

"My sister?" he said, confused. "What has Gina got to do with this?" He spread the newspaper across her desk and pointed to the headlines in the business section: "INTERNATIONAL RUMORED TO BUY EMPRESS HOTELS."

"Oh, *that*." Caasi sighed with relief. "I thought you were talking about . . ."

"I know what you thought," he shouted. "I want to ask you about this article. Is it true?"

She gestured toward the chair on the other side of her desk. "Will you sit down?" she requested calmly, her even words belying her pounding heart. "We need to talk, and there's no better time than the present."

Blake lowered himself into the soft leather chair, but he sat on the edge of the seat as if ready to spring up at the slightest provocation.

"Well?" he demanded again. "Is it true?"

"Yes," she said, confirming his suspicions. "But I'm only selling eight hotels. I'm keeping the Portland Empress and the Seaside Empress."

"Caasi." He groaned in frustration. "Do you know what you're doing?"

"Yes." She nodded. "I've never been more sure of anything in my life. I don't have the time to manage the hotels and everything else."

"Everything else? What?" he demanded. "What could possibly be more important to you than Crane Enterprises?"

Sitting opposite him, Caasi watched his face intently as she spoke. "A baby," she murmured softly.

"A baby," he exploded and shot to his feet.

Caasi closed her eyes and emitted a bittersweet groan. "Blake, I wanted to have a nice logical discussion with you. But if you insist on overreacting like this, then I'm simply going to have to ask you to leave."

"You don't say things like that and expect me to react as if you've asked for the sugar bowl."

"Okay, okay," she agreed with limited patience. "When you've cooled down I'd like to have a calm, rational discussion."

He took a package of cigarettes from his pocket and lit one, inhaling deeply on it. "Are you pregnant?" He centered his attention on the trail of smoke that penetrated the air.

"Not yet."

"Not yet?" Hard impatience showed in the set of his mouth.

Caasi lowered her gaze and struggled to keep a firm grip on her composure. "I've met with a real estate agent and have started looking at houses. I don't want my baby growing up in a hotel the way I did."

Blake straightened in the chair, his back ramrod stiff.

"I've also talked with an attorney, and he's drawing up the necessary papers. I think . . . the father . . . should have some rights, but I'd be foolish not to protect myself and the baby legally."

Blake's face was hard, his eyes blazing. Yet he was pale, as if his grip on his temper was fragile. "And the father?" he asked curtly.

"Yes, well . . ." Caasi felt the muscles of her throat tighten as the words slipped out. "I'd like you to be my baby's father."

Chapter Ten

Blake's razor-sharp gaze ripped into her. "What did you say?"

Caasi had trouble meeting his eyes. "You heard me right."

Blake propelled himself out of the chair and stalked to the far side of the room. "Have you seen a doctor?" He ground out the question, his back to her.

"No, not yet. I didn't feel that would be necessary until I was fairly certain I was pregnant," she explained tightly.

Blake swiveled around, his brow knit with questioning concern. "I'm not talking about that kind of doctor."

"Honestly, Blake. Do you think I need a psychiatrist?" A nervous smile played at the corners of her mouth.

"Yes," he insisted, "quite frankly, that's exactly what I think. You've been working too hard."

Caasi's spirits sank and she lowered her head. Her fingers toyed with a stack of papers on her desk. "I'm not working any harder now than I have for the past five years."

"Exactly." His hand sliced through the air.

"Blake, the Empress has nothing to do with this. I woke up, that's all. I've decided I want something more out of life than money and an empty suite." She didn't elaborate that he was the one responsible for awakening her. "I'm a woman with a woman's desires. Is it so wrong to want to be a mother? I can assure you I'll be a good one." She inhaled deeply. "June says I'm a natural with the baby and I'd make—."

"Why pick me?" he interrupted, a grim set to his jaw.

"Why not?" she said and shrugged. The heat seeped into her face, reddening her cheeks. "You're tall, good-looking, and possess certain characteristics I admire." Nervously she stood up and walked around to the front of the desk. Leaning back against the flat top, she crossed her arms.

"Just how do you propose to get pregnant? By osmosis?" Blake taunted.

"No . . . of course not," she stammered. "Listen, Blake, I'm not doing a very good job of explaining this. I really wish I hadn't said anything. At least, not until I'd heard from the lawyer. But aside from anything else, I'd like you to know I'm willing to make this venture worth your while."

His mouth twisted into a cynical smile. "You don't

have enough money to pay me for what you're asking. I'd like to tell you what to do with your proposition, Cupcake, but your face would burn for a week." Slowly he turned and walked to the door.

"Don't go, Blake. Please."

His hand on the doorknob, he turned; his gaze was concentrated on her, disturbing her even more. "There's nothing you can say. Good-bye, Cupcake."

Just the way he said it made her blood run cold. His voice expressed so many things in those few words. Frustration. Disappointment. Contempt. Disbelief.

Caasi sagged against the desk as the door closed. Blake couldn't be feeling any more confused than she was. He had been angry. Blazingly angry. She'd seen him express a myriad of emotions over the years. And plenty of anger. But never like this. This kind of anger went beyond raised voices and lost tempers. This time it came from Blake's heart.

The thought of working was almost impossible. Caasi tried for the remainder of the morning, but her concentration drifted, and every page seemed to mirror Blake's look as he walked out the door. At lunchtime she announced to Louise that she didn't know when she'd be back. Louise rounded her eyes with frustration but said nothing.

Caasi let herself into the penthouse suite and slowly sauntered around the empty quarters. She shouldn't have approached Blake that day. Even the most naïve business graduate would have recognized that this wasn't the time to propose anything to him. He'd been upset even before she'd opened her mouth. Her sense of timing couldn't have been more off kilter. That wasn't like her. She knew better.

Staring out the window, Caasi blinked uncertainly. She needed to get away. Think. Reconsider.

After changing out of her smart linen business suit into maroon cords and a pink sweater, she took her car out of the garage and drove around for awhile. It was true that she wanted a baby. But what she hadn't realized until that morning was that she wanted Blake's child. If he wouldn't agree, then she would have to abandon the idea completely.

She had to talk to Blake and make him understand. All the way to Gresham, she practiced what she wanted to say, the assurances she would give him. Nothing in her life had ever been so important.

His driveway was empty when she turned into it. She had counted on his being there. Just as she climbed out of her car, it started to rain. Staring at the skies in defeat, Caasi raised the collar of her jacket and hurried up the back steps, pounding on the door on the off chance he was inside. Nothing.

Rushing back to her car, she climbed inside and listened to the pelting rain dance on the roof. An arc of lightning flashed across the dark sky. *Wonderful,* she reflected disconsolately. Even nature responded to Blake's moods.

Ten minutes passed and it seemed like ten years. But Caasi was determined to stay until she'd had the chance to explain things to Blake.

Half an hour later, when the storm was beginning to abate, she got out of the car a second time. Maybe Blake had left his back door unlocked and she could go inside.

The door was tightly locked, but Caasi found a key under a ceramic flowerpot. It looked old and slightly rusted. Briefly Caasi wondered if Blake even knew it was there. After several minutes spent trying to work the key into the lock, she managed to open the door.

Wiping her feet on the mat, she let herself into the kitchen. Blake's dirty breakfast dishes were on the table and she carried them to the sink. It looked as if he'd been reading the morning paper, found the article about the rumored sale of the Empress, and rushed out the door, newspaper in hand.

To fill the time, she leafed through several magazines. But nothing held her interest, so she straightened up the living room and ran warm, sudsy water into the kitchen sink to wash the breakfast dishes. She had just finished scrubbing the frying pan when she heard a car in the driveway.

Her heart thumped as though she'd just run a marathon when Blake walked in the door. Turning, her hands braced on the edge of the sink behind her, Caasi smiled weakly.

"Who let you in?"

Involuntarily, Caasi flinched at the cutting edge in his voice.

"There was a key under the flowerpot." Her voice nearly failed her. Turning back to the sink, she jerked the kitchen towel from the drawer and started drying the few dishes she'd washed. At least she could hide how badly her hands were shaking.

"Okay, we'll abort that how and go directly to why. Why are you here?" The dry sarcasm in his voice knotted her stomach.

"Would you like a cup of coffee?" she asked brightly. "I know I would."

"No!" he nearly shouted. "I don't want any coffee.

What I'd like is a simple explanation." His narrowed gaze swung to her as she took a mug from the cupboard and helped herself to the fresh pot of coffee she'd made.

"Caasi." The tone of his voice as he spoke her name revealed the depth of his frustration.

Pulling out a chair, she sat down, her eyes issuing a silent invitation for him to do the same.

He ignored her and leaned against the kitchen counter.

She didn't look at him as she spoke. "You once accused me of having ink in my veins. At the time you were right. But the ink is gone and there's blood flowing there now." Briefly her gray eyes slid to him. His stance didn't encourage her to continue.

"So?" His arms were crossed as if to block her out. He drew his head back, pride dictating the indifference he so vividly portrayed.

"So?" she repeated with bitter mockery. *"You* did this to me. You're the one responsible. . . ."

Blake straightened slightly. "Does that make it my duty to fall in with these looney plans of yours? Do you have any idea of how crazy you sound? You want to pay me to father your child, so you can be a mother. What in heaven's name do you have against marriage?"

"Nothing. I . . . I think marriage is wonderful."

"Then if you're so hot for a family, why don't we get married?"

She stiffened with angry pride as she met his glare. "Is this a proposal?"

"Yes," he snapped.

Caasi felt as if someone had punched her in the stomach, effectively knocking the oxygen from her lungs. Tears brimmed in her eyes.

"Well?" His voice softened perceptibly.

One tear slid down her drawn face and she wiped it aside with the tips of her fingers. "Every girl dreams about having a man ask her to marry him. I never thought my proposal would be shouted at me from across a kitchen."

"I'm not exactly in a romantic mood. Do you want to get married or don't you?" he barked. "And while we're on the subject, let's get something else straight. We'll live right here in this house and on my income. Whatever money is yours will be put into a trust fund for the children."

A soft curtain of hair fell forward to cover her face as she stared into the steaming coffee. "My mother died before I knew her," she began weakly. "Maybe if she'd lived I would know a better way to say these things. To me, marriage means more than producing children. There's love and commitment and a hundred different things I don't even know how to explain. The quiet communication I witnessed between your mother and father. That look in Burt's eyes as June was delivering their child. Do you see what I'm trying to say?"

Blake was quiet for so long, she wondered if he'd heard her. "Maybe as time goes by you could learn to love me," Blake said with slow deliberation. "I think we should give it a try."

"Learn to love you?" Caasi repeated incredulously. "I love you already." She raised her eyes to his, her gaze level and clear. "I don't want any baby unless it's yours. I don't want any other man but you . . . ever."

In the next instant, she was hauled out of the chair and into his arms. "You love me?" Roughly he pushed the hair from her eyes, as if he had to see it himself, couldn't believe what she was saying and had to read it in her face.

Her hands were braced against his chest. "Of course I do. Could I have made it any more obvious in Seaside?" Her lashes fluttered closed as she struggled to disguise the pain that his rejection still had the power to inflict. "But you . . . you . . ."

"I know what I did," he interrupted, a grim set to his mouth. "I walked out. It was the hardest thing I'd ever done in my life, but I turned away and left you." He released her and twined his fingers through his hair. "I was half a breath from telling you how much I loved you. Then I heard you say that you were absolving me from any responsibility. Here I was ready to give you my heart and you were talking to me like a one-night stand."

"Oh, Blake." She moaned, lifting the hair from her forehead with one hand. "I wanted you to understand that I didn't expect anything of you. You didn't have to love me, not when I loved you so much."

Tenderly, his eyes caressed her. "How can any two people misunderstand each other the way we have?"

Sadly, Caasi shook her head. "Why did you resign? Why did you leave when I wanted you so desperately to stay?"

He took her back into his arms, and his lips softly brushed her cheek. "Because loving you and working with you were becoming impossible. I've loved you almost from the moment you floated into your father's office that day. I kept waiting for you to wake up to that fact. Then one day I realized you never would."

"Why didn't you say something? Why didn't you let me know?"

"Caasi, I couldn't have been any more obvious. All the times I made excuses to touch you, be with you. Anything. But you were so caught up in Crane Enterprises you didn't notice. And, to be truthful, your money intimidated me. One day I decided: why torture myself anymore? You were already married to the company, and I was never going to be rich enough for you to believe I wasn't attracted to you for your money."

"But, Blake, I didn't think that. Not once."

"But then, you didn't guess I loved you either."

Smiling, Caasi slid her arms over his shoulders and looked at him with all the love in her heart shining from the blue-gray depths of her eyes. "But now that I know, Blake Sherrill, I'm not letting you go. Not for a minute."

Tenderly he kissed her as if she were a fragile flower and held her close as if he'd never release her.

"I love you so much." She curled tighter into his embrace. "And, Blake, we're going to have the most beautiful children."

"Yes," he murmured, his lips seeking hers. "But not for a year. I want you to myself for that long. Understood?"

"Oh, yes," she agreed eagerly, her eyes glowing with the soft light of happiness. "Anything you say."

Five months later Caasi stood on the back porch as Blake drove into the driveway. Even after three months of marriage, just seeing her husband climb out of the car at the end of the day produced a wealth of emotions.

"Hi—how was your afternoon?" she greeted him, wrapping her arms around his neck and kissing him ardently. She worked mornings at the Empress but gradually was turning her responsibilities over to Blake so that the time would come when she could pursue some of the things she wanted.

Lifting her off the floor, Blake swung her around, his mouth locating the sensitive area at the hollow of her throat, knowing the tingling reaction he'd evoke.

"You're being mighty brave for five-thirty in the afternoon," she teased.

"It doesn't seem to matter what time of the day it is, I don't think I'll ever stop wanting you," he whispered in her ear. "Fifty years from now, I'll probably be chasing you around the bedroom." His voice was deep and emotion-filled.

"I don't think you'll have to chase too hard."

"Good thing," he said, teasing also, and set his briefcase aside so he could hold her tightly against him. "Your cooking is improving, because whatever it is smells delicious."

"Yes; that reminds me." Caasi groaned and broke from his embrace. "I have good news and bad news. Which do you want first?"

Blake's eyes narrowed fractionally. "Knowing you, I think I'd better hear the bad news first."

"Promise you won't get angry?"

"I'm not making any promises." He pulled her back into his arms and nuzzled her throat playfully.

Giggling and happy, Caasi blurted out, "The bad news is I burnt the roast. The good news is I went out and got Kentucky Fried Chicken."

"Caasi, that's twice this month." Blake groaned, but there was no anger in the way his eyes caressed her.

"That's not all," she added, lowering her eyes. "Honey, I tried, but I can't make Ekalb into a decent name for a boy or a girl."

Blake laughed. "What are you talking about now?"

"Your name spelled backwards, silly. I wanted to name the baby after you, and Ekalb just isn't going to do it."

A stunned silence fell over the room. "Baby?" Blake repeated. "What baby?"

"The one right here." She took his hand and pressed it against her flat stomach. "I know you said a year, but eight months from now it will be almost that long."

"Caasi," Blake murmured as if he couldn't believe what he was hearing. "Why didn't you say something sooner?"

"I couldn't. Not until I was sure. Are you angry?"

"Angry?" He chuckled. "No, never that. Just surprised, that's all." His smile was filled with an intense satisfaction as he pulled her into his arms.

Closing her eyes, Caasi slid her arms around her husband's neck and released a contented sigh as she drew his mouth to hers.

Romantic Seasonal Stories...

Four new love stories with special festive themes are presented in one seasonal volume.

The Man from Pine Mountain
Lisa Jackson

Naughty or Nice
Emilie Richards

Holiday Homecoming
Joan Hohl

A Kiss for Mr Scrooge
Lucy Gordon

PUBLISHED NOVEMBER 1994   PRICED £4.50

SILHOUETTE

Available from WH Smith, John Menzies, Volume One, Forbuoys, Martins, Woolworths, Tesco, Asda, Safeway and other paperback stockists.

SILHOUETTE

Desire

COMING NEXT MONTH

HAVEN'S CALL Robin Elliott

Man of the Month

Call Shannon had been forced out of retirement to investigate Haven Larson. But could he uncover the young widow's secrets without revealing his own?

SALTY AND FELICIA Lass Small

Fabulous Brown Brothers

The last thing Salty Brown wanted—but the one thing he *needed*—was a woman. He had his hands full already with his three adopted sons. But he had reckoned without the determination of Felicia Strode!

BEWILDERED Jennifer Greene

The Connor Men

Michael Connor was every woman's fantasy: tall, honest, handsome. And the intensity of his first kiss had left Simone hungry for more...

THE PIRATE PRINCESS Suzanne Simms

Hazards Inc.

Melina Morgan had left her sedate librarian image behind her. Bold, sexy and adventurous, she had set her sights on Nick Hazard and was determined to get her man!

SUBSTITUTE WIFE Anne Marie Winston

Tom Hayes needed a mother for his young family and Tannis Carlson seemed a good candidate for the role. But Tannis hadn't been a substitute wife very long before she was dreaming of being the real thing...

UNCAGED Lucy Gordon

Megan Anderson had spent three years learning to hate Daniel Keller. His unwitting testimony had sentenced an innocent woman to prison, robbing Megan of her son and all but destroying her life. Now she was free and determined to make him pay!

COMING NEXT MONTH FROM
▼ SILHOUETTE

Sensation

A thrilling mix of passion, adventure and drama

PROMISES IN THE NIGHT Barbara Bretton
TARGET OF OPPORTUNITY Justine Davis
HEROES GREAT AND SMALL Marie Ferrarella
A WALK ON THE WILD SIDE Kathleen Korbel

Intrigue

*Danger, deception and desire—
new from Silhouette...*

BLOOD TIES Laurel Pace
MIDNIGHT MASQUE Jenna Ryan
HAUNTED Patricia Rosemoor
LEGAL TENDER Kelsey Roberts

Special Edition

Satisfying romances packed with emotion

DAUGHTER OF THE BRIDE Christine Flynn
COUNTDOWN Lindsay McKenna
ALWAYS Ginna Gray
BABY IN THE MIDDLE Marie Ferrarella
A BRIDE FOR HUNTER Pat Warren
A FAMILY TO CHERISH Colleen Norman

Have a romantic Christmas with Silhouette

Three new Sensation novels that feature the love and passions at Christmas time are contained in this attractive gift pack.

A Christmas Marriage
Dallas Schulze

A Country Christmas
Jackie Weger

A Cowboy for Christmas
Anne McAllister

PUBLISHED NOVEMBER 1994   PRICED £5.85

SILHOUETTE

Available from WH Smith, John Menzies, Volume One, Forbuoys, Martins, Woolworths, Tesco, Asda, Safeway and other paperback stockists.